THE FALL GAUNTLET:

VOLUME 1

BOOKS 1 - 3

J. A. MERKEL

THE FALL GAUNTLET:

BEAR

BOOK ONE

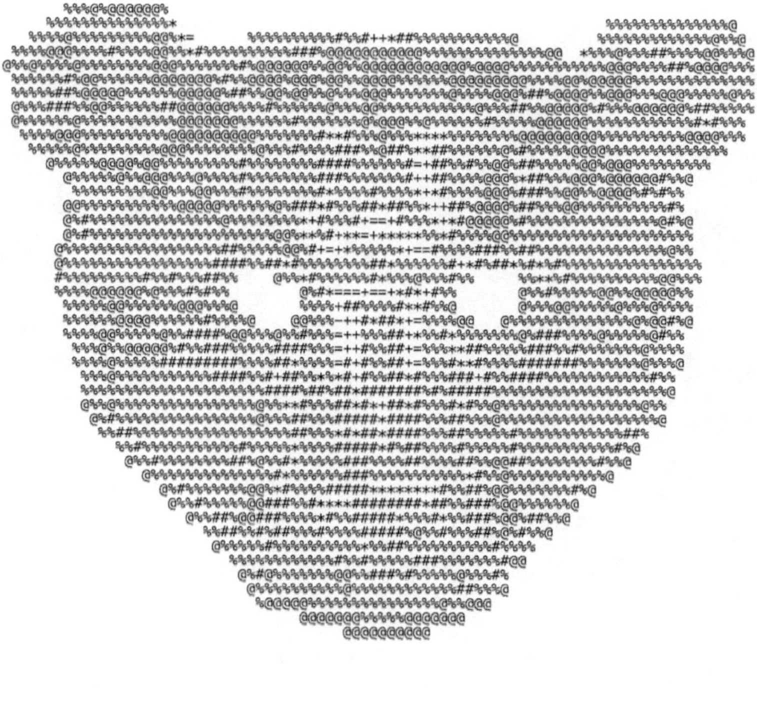

A Worlds Apart Media Book
PUBLISHING HISTORY
Worlds Apart paperback edition / January 2024

ISBN: 979-8-9888120-4-3
Printed in the United States of America

The Fall Gauntlet: Volume 1

Book 1: BEAR

Book 2: RAT

Book 3: CHRYSIX

For Jude,

No matter which universes we find ourselves in, I know time and again, we'll be brothers every time.

BEAR

It is said that the bear disappeared from Calypso before many of the first animals; that among all the Originals, it sought out wisdom from the gods and goddesses before all others.

Would it be impossible to imagine that a creature so carefully crafted by the Dei would eventually seek out its creators? Or was the bear searching for something else?

Totem scholars believe that the bear never left our planet, that it is sleeping within the hollow of a great tree, waiting for its human champion to wake it from its slumber and bring protection to the land.

When the bear appears to you in a dream, listen to its steady breathing. Feel the beat of its one true and vicious heart. Learn the location of its sacrifice.

That is when the bear will awaken. That is when the bear lives inside you.

The Book of Totems, Bear

ONE

In my nightmares, Soren and I are running. We're always running, but it's never fast enough. No one in my family can ever run fast enough.

On the morning of my final match, D rushes down the tunnel leading to my holding cell with the decisive and energetic footsteps I've come to know so well. She isn't supposed to be here, especially at five in the morning hours before my match, but I've stopped trying to figure out the Crown or anything about how the gods and goddesses work.

I put my lynx mask down on my desk and meet her at the door as her echoing steps die to nothing. She's out of breath, more hurried and rattled than I've seen her. "Has something happened? Am I still supposed to fight today?"

Pre-dawn light filters through the one barred window and casts deep shadows on her pale face as our planet tilts and opens itself to our star for the day. Another day of judgment. Her emerald-green eyes are hot with some unspoken pain, but her words are like ice. She is the one to carry the news of my brother, Soren, to me.

"He's been training for the gauntlet, Benji," D says, catching her breath. "He's the one you have to fight."

Now I'm the breathless one.

Sometimes, you train for the better part of your life so you can save your mother from her off-world prison, and other times, you have to fight to the death against your own flesh and blood to free her.

I always thought Mom being arrested for treason and taken away was the beginning of the end, but in time I learned we would all pay for our sins: Dad, for the medicines we'd stolen to heal his infected and rotting leg from his accident at the mines; Soren, for breaking the leg of the Crown; and me, for orchestrating the heist.

That's the Crown for you—just when you think they've taken everything, they take more. And now they're doing it again.

Dad used to say that the Fall Gauntlet tournament was the Crown's way of maintaining public order by having people fight for what they believe in, while also pleasing the Dei, our all-knowing gods and goddesses—wherever they're supposed to be—but I'm beginning to think it's about something else.

The creators have been waiting for today, for the strongest fighter and totem animal to claim victory and rule over Harvest. At least for the next four years, until the next tournament happens and the cycle starts all over again. They'll grant the victor one wish, but—

Soren's been training for the gauntlet?

My tongue feels like it's fallen down into my throat, but then I get the words out. "That wonderful and insightful piece of information would have been good . . . oh, I don't know—seven years ago?" That's when Soren and I were separated from one another. Dad went to prison and we never heard from him again. Soren was sent to the mines at just eight years old to take Dad's place. Since I was skilled at ciantechnology by then, based on the contraptions I had made, they sent me to the inner circle to apprentice under Master Gherus, where I would make weapons and tech for the Crown.

D winces, swallowing the words I know she was ready to say, as she presses fingers against her temples. I know this is hard for her too. We've grown close during these last few months. She's been my confidante, a source of strength when I return to my cell, bringer of food, and speaker of mostly soothing words. This isn't her fault. The last thing I want is for her to feel bad about something she did or didn't tell me.

My entire family is being torn apart by the Crown, I'm about to battle my little brother to the death, and here I am worried about one of the Crown guards' feelings. Granted, she's not just any guard, but still—classic Benji move. This is probably why the Crown can control me with the promise of freeing my mother. Feelings.

"I'm sorry, Benji. I didn't know until now," D says. "One of the other guards was mouthing off, and they were going on and on about the bear champion, and they let the name Soren slip. I know you talked about him to me before. He's your final opponent." The words tumble out of her mouth like she doesn't have enough time. She steals a glance behind her. Maybe she doesn't.

"That doesn't get easier the second time you say it," I say.

"Benji, pull out. You can't fight against your brother— you can't beat the bear!"

D already knows that deserters are executed, so I don't remind her and instead indulge her small moment of hysteria. The Crown would never allow Soren or me to leave the gauntlet because our nation needs a champion. A

3

victorious bear means something very different for the people of the land than a victorious lynx.

I pick up my heavy lynx mask from my cot. I feel better holding it, being close to it—it helps me see what others cannot and has always been my key to victory.

Ignoring the fact that D thinks Soren can beat me in a fight, I say, "I need to see him. It's hard to believe you. That it's him. That he's here, fighting in this tournament too." I'm back at the cell door, looking into D's eyes, hoping there's some mistake.

Soren.

My only brother.

It's amazing what neural connections can do, because the second that I accept this news about Soren, my world opens to his presence, and memories of when we were last together rush towards me.

Light from the window skitters across the holding cell floor, but in another time, I'm seeing guards come through our door after one knock, as though these two realities are superimposed on one another.

Soren and I are escaping from a window. I'm waiting for Soren to land, to hurry up. Not hurried enough. A guard is intercepting us, grabbing me by the wrist, but then I'm turning his weight against him, bringing him down.

There's a rush of exhilaration, the unspeakable satisfaction of besting someone I hate, someone who had already taken my mother away, and then the guard is on his feet, and my throat is in his hand, my back crushed against the stone wall, feet dangling, helpless. Soren is dropping down, finally. His eyes hold a golden glint, that first sign of rage that I knew even then would be our family's undoing.

Soren is punching once, twice, three times, and I'm telling him no, demanding that he stop. Soren is pausing, considering. I'm outmaneuvering the guard again, shooting my gripclaw into the wooden post above as I lasso his wrists and send him skyward, his bulky frame jerking off the ground like a fish on a hook.

The cool morning air is rushing past us as we sprint through the long and winding labyrinth that leads to home. Thoughts arrive, so many thoughts, a premonition, something warning me.

We should have been more careful.

We arrive home, throw open the door, excited to give Dad the medicine we've stolen, then—a silence so heavy it can crush your soul.

Two henchmen and a gauntlet juror named Harmeny stand in our home. Harmeny is calling us thieves, telling us that thieves do not go unpunished under her watch. I'm thinking—knowing—that we should have never let the guard in the street see us.

There's a pang in my stomach for what Soren did, and I'm getting a sickening feeling, my stomach twisting into unrecognizable shapes, for what he is about to do.

He couldn't prevent it. Neither of us could prevent it. But Soren made sure to leave his mark.

My mind goes black.

"Benji, they say he kills people with one swing of his club," D says.

I don't respond.

I've heard stories and whispers over the years that Soren became angry and stupid, a ball of trapped energy refusing to learn how to read or return to the society he'd known.

It's hard to picture my brother and what he'd look like now, if he'd grown into a similar version of me, or if he'd reached the size and height Mom and Dad thought he would, tall and broad like a sailor. Like Poppy.

If he is the bear, he might be huge. I've never seen the bear, but I've heard about him. Part of me knew this is how it would end up, but the fact that my opponent is Soren is a shock I still can't process.

I wrack my brain for the lore behind the bear champion, trying to decipher what this matchup—lynx versus bear—will mean.

D is crying, and her hands are shaking as she presses them against her chest. Her tears are silent but carry years of pain over the Crown destroying lives like we are all just pawns on a chess board—expendable and insignificant.

The urge to shout at someone, something, anything, takes over. I want to tell D she's lying, that this is all a big trick, because what more could the Crown do to torture their citizens? What more could they do to torture me that they haven't already done?

They could feed me lies about my family, about the possibility of saving them, then pit me against my brother with only minutes to process the ordeal. It's been ten years since they took my mother, seven since they took my father and brother. Ten years of wondering and dreaming and wishing for a way to be with my family again, and this is how it happens.

"Are you in danger?" I ask her, aware of movement from new pieces in this grand chess game the Crown has constructed.

"Not that I know of." D shakes her head, brushing off my question. She looks up at me with bloodshot eyes. "How can the Crown be so cruel?"

I don't answer. I have to remain neutral, especially this close to my final match. A win means my wish will be granted and I can finally save Mom.

I'm so close to this victory, but now the Crown has chucked a rather large wrench into the works, clogging up and complicating what I've spent so many years building. I know I have to make a decision.

"What are you going to do, Benji?" D's eyes are bright with half-shed tears.

I hold up my mask as though it holds the answers that I need. With microchips and photosensors embedded into the interior, handiwork that I once learned while apprenticing for Master Gherus within the castle walls, the mask feels familiar, like it is the only ally I have in this fight.

Gherus taught me that I could become someone else with technology's help. By learning the principles of physics, by training to strengthen my muscles and perform maneuvers that would surprise and take down my opponents, I learned that I, too, could become a champion and make a wish to save the ones I loved. And if I didn't win, I'd die trying.

Placing the mask on my face will activate the aura field and release fission elements so that the mask's photon-receptors can create a more realistic image of a lynx. Once the organix have finished pixelating the holoskin, and my own internal system has calibrated to the mask's, integration will be complete. Removing my mask will result in immediate execution, since the identities of the fighters must always remain secret, so I'll need to figure out a way to show Soren—in case he doesn't already know—that he's fighting against his dear older brother.

Sure, easy enough.

The only other rule of the gauntlet is that there can be only one champion. There are no draws.

"I'll do what I've always done," I say. "Defeat whatever the Crown throws at me."

I don't share with D what I'm really thinking.

I have no idea what to do.

TWO

Even from down here in the tunnels, I can hear the raucous stadium above me erupt with pre-match excitement; the thumping of sticks on goat-skinned drums, the boisterous, drunken laughter, and the wild, shrieking applause from the thousands of spectators create a collective and thunderous orchestra.

Several victories advanced me from the grunt rounds into the champion rounds. I'd chosen Gherus as my sponsor, so he was allowed to visit me at the time. Face to face, his eyes were soft and on the verge of tears. In the beginning, I was just an orphan on house arrest, the son of traitors using his skills to pay his debts to the Crown, but that was not what I was to Gherus by the end of my apprenticeship. A kind of orphan himself, we'd found that family was not only dictated by bloodline.

There was indecision in Gherus's eyes that day, but he was never too conflicted to give me advice that would save my life. "You have to consider what will happen in your final match, should you make it that far," he'd said. "There are many possibilities to consider."

"There's only one possibility," I'd said. "I'm going to save my mom."

Gherus dropped his gaze and his tone, his rapid speech revealing his anxiousness. "This isn't about what you want, Benji. This is, and has always been, about the Crown. This is about the world they've built and what they want. You are a pawn."

"A pawn that has almost reached the other side of the board," I'd said, slamming my fists against the cell door.

"We all have people we love," Gherus had said. "Do you think you're the only person looking to save someone?"

Now, on the other side of these walls, Soren is waiting for his platform to take him to the gauntlet, just as I am waiting for mine. It's strange to think how much our lives have run parallel to each other, and yet I know nothing about him. Perhaps his time in the mines has made him a fierce, indestructible fighter. All these thoughts come to me in the dim light of the tunnels, as I stave off the scent of cool, musty air. I have traversed these tunnels dozens of times and as usual, I am alone.

I step onto my platform, but it does nothing. The hyrotech on the wall glows a neon orange to form an image of a mask. I hold my inactive lynx mask in my left hand, as though putting it on is acceptance of this fight.

News of Soren has my mind doing all sorts of things because now I'm thinking of the day I first entered the temple to speak my sacrifice to the Dei, in the hopes that I would be chosen for the tournament. They say the Dei choose their champions through the masks, Calypson vessels holding a portion of the gods' and goddesses' true power.

I'd lifted the dense, cold mask in my hands and stared into the lifeless eyes of the lynx, knowing that the totem animal was the closest match to my own spirit—a being of evolution and scientific discovery. If only I had known then that Soren would enter the temple at the hour of the bear, I could have prepared better for today.

My nerves were steel that day because I had nothing left to lose. Entering the tournament was the closest I'd ever get to the Dei, and winning was the only way I'd ever save Mom. I was either becoming the lynx now or never.

I placed the mask on my face while reciting the lynx's words and waited. Within the dark cave of the ancient device, the world became quiet, and then the Dei heard the sacrifice of my heart: my own life in exchange for the age-old tournament, and they—no, the lynx—chose me. The strength I felt then was otherworldly. The lynx's powers of precognition awakened and the temple exploded into a cosmic universe of probabilities that, at the time, I had no clue how to interpret.

Three months later, I understand my mask's abilities very well. As long as I live, the mask is codified to me and only I can wear it. Together, on this day of final judgment, only the lynx and I can activate this platform to take us to the arena. There are no stand-ins.

The creators have written it in the stars . . . or something like that.

Now or never, Benji.

The Crown will kill me if I don't engage, so I put it on like the good little fighter they want me to be. My body tightens like a hamstring in that first moment of mask transition like it always does, as my neurotransmitters stabilize and the o-tech calibrates to my own internal system; thousands of microsensors make contact with my skin, syncing with my brainwaves and locking into place with the larger structures of my meaty brain like parts of a two-pieced puzzle. I'm clenching my fists and gnashing my teeth as the human-mask integration roils on, the process combining genetics, psychohistory, and physiology, and the mask's superhuman abilities of prediction are plugged directly into my consciousness. The mask's boosted effect on my physiology, resulting in increased strength, agility, and reaction time, envelops my body like a laser scan and then it's over, burning off me in a wave of invisible heat. I feel thirty pounds stronger, but lithe like a lynx.

I grab my gem staff off the wall in front of me, the weapon paired with the lynx since the beginning of the gauntlet, centuries before I was born. Anyone could pick it up and use it, but only organix activation—when the totem mask and its human match unite—unlocks its true potential. Nanoparticles coalesce to fortify the staff as it reaches its full height at six feet to match my own, the gemstone held in the crook at the end pulsing a cyan blue. The spark core is a thundercloud of potential energy, branching and spreading like the effervescent veins of leaves under glowlight. It doesn't seem like much when you're fighting against armored enemies with broadswords or serrated claws for hands, but the kinetic force that is created with movement can deliver a finishing blow with the right amount of power and technique.

The neon light in front of me morphs from orange to green and the system says in its feminine lilt, "Lynx identified. May you see the truth, always and forever." My platform rises.

The stadium floor opens above me as·harsh sunlight presses against my suit. Now that my mask is on, the crowd will see the image and likeness of my lynx persona as the mask's micro hairs grow denser and my ears elongate until they form pointed tips. My skintight pants, lightweight boots—more like sandals strapped around my heels and calves—and a breathable mesh tunic fitted firmly to my body all help improve my aerodynamics.

The cacophony of sound is both dulled from within the cave of the mask on my face and augmented, voices and battle chants echoing through the cavernous expanse of sky above me. The humid air envelops me in its warm embrace as sweat runs down the back of my neck, and tiny hairs prickle against my lightweight garments. I can't stop the adrenaline now rushing through me as thousands of people wait for their new champion and an understanding of what this next Harvest will mean.

The last time the gauntlet took place, I was only thirteen. The eagle had claimed victory, so Harvest followed the lore of our mighty winged predecessor.

The eagle summoned eastern winds meant to carry new life, pollination from other nations to grow new crops and trees and flowers. The winds would also power windmills that the Crown would build on farms. All that had happened when the eagle defeated the badger, a champion of grit, and a symbol of what it means to fight against something bigger than oneself.

It was easy to see which one of the two the Crown favored. I'll always remember how the badger fought that day, how it tried to break through the defensive winged shields of the eagle, only to be blown back again and again, until it could fight no more. The eagle delivered a finishing blow with its razor-thin wing blades, and the bloody, battered badger lost its head in a bloodcurdling moment that I'll never be able to unsee. At thirteen, I should have been more disturbed by it, but it felt like the natural progression of things. Violence seemed and still seems like the only way to get what you want in our cruel world.

And now they're turning flesh and blood against each other.

This death match of lynx versus bear is twisting my stomach into knots, and my platform has almost reached the stadium. Under the cloudless lapis-blue sky, spectators are clinking their drinks and drowning their sorrows in the veiled hope that their lives will be different tomorrow once there is a new champion.

A bear victory would spell four years of security and steady harvest in preparation for the long winter. The bear symbolizes a close connection to the ground, dirt, and soil, the land that feeds. The bear signifies overall protection and is, ironically, maternal in essence. Last I'd seen Soren, he was about as unmotherly as one could get. It makes sense, though, why people believe in the bear. The mother of mammals also represents protection against outside forces, and we've always been a nation all too aware of the rebel clans to the west. A victory from the bear during any other gauntlet would be preferred, but not when it means my own death.

I can't allow the bear to win.

The morning sun beats down on me like a thousand hot needles, but I keep my eyes closed for now, focusing on my breath, on the nuances of sound and smell that will be my allies in this fight.

I need to focus on myself—on the lynx.

This is the first time the totem has become one of the sixteen champions. I represent a new path for the people of New Phasia: science. But since people's lives are on the line, novelty is synonymous with death. To most people, science is a scary word because it's something they don't understand. I have a hunch that the Crown has orchestrated this shielding of knowledge, but I have neither the time nor know-how to expose it. And besides, that isn't my destiny. If I win, it is the Crown's duty to generate new tech and identify new talent across the nation.

The lynx is the totem of high intellect and a desire to understand all that is known and unknown, which clashes like metal on metal with the people of New Phasia, who believe in working in the fields with their hands in the dirt.

My photon mask buzzes with a near-imperceptible electromagnetic frequency, and I'm bound to it then. It hugs my face like a mother I never really got to hold. Gauntlet champions have always been masked so the technology has been around for ages, but most people cannot recreate it, much less understand even the most basic principles of how phospho-imaging works.

The eyes of the lynx see the greater mysteries of life. As is my ritual of reviewing the lore of my opponent's champion, followed by my own, I touch the side of my photon mask and activate the hypo-ocular receptors built into the motherboard. The world explodes in a kaleidoscope of teals, oranges, indigoes, yellows and reds. The sudden shift is jarring, but I'm used to it now and can stomach the additional transition much easier than the first time. Light filters through, and the colors settle into layers as I parse them out into the reality unfolding before me.

I'm almost at the platform, which is raised one hundred feet off the ground. I peer down and see the spikes jutting into the air like giant shark teeth as deadly as a Megalodon's, the Crown's final assurance that only one champion survives.

My platform stops.

One more step across the gap and my final match begins. There he is. My heart catches in my throat, like a serpent trying to swallow a creature too large for it. The air is dry with heat, oppressive. Through the mask's openings, I take small sips of air with my mouth, exhaling through my nostrils. The twisting of my stomach tightens, and I am a mangled knot of fear and anger and love. The bear stands before me, and I don't even need to see behind the mask to know. I know it like the blood that runs through my veins, down to the marrow of my bones. Call it an energy.

D was right. My final match is against a brother I haven't seen or known in seven years.

My final match is against Soren.

The last time I saw Soren fight we were in our house in the Syphon District, which bordered the inner district, and was home to peasants like me and my family. Soren was a thin, raggedy child who stole food to keep up. It's hard to believe that I'm related to the fifteen-year-old in a bear mask facing me down like I'm the one who's taken his family away. I wonder if he knows what I know.

When I look at him and begin to intuit what he will do, my visual receptors activate, and I see what no one else can. The crowd is witnessing two masked humans representing both a bear and a lynx, human-shaped with the ability to walk upright, but phospho-imaged to imitate those beasts, our masks morphing and sprouting hair, and our gauntlets growing retractable claws and fur. For as long as I focus my cerebral energy on seeing beyond the blurred illusion of holoskin that masks his features, I'll be able to see the real Soren underneath. I only need a moment.

Soren is big. He's at least a head taller than me, and broader in the shoulders. His forearms and legs are hairy, as though he's become part bear himself. My mask's main ability is probability precognition, meaning I can intuit mini futures based on probable outcomes in order to inform my choices. Its function is based on a complicated framework of neural pathways that are synced to the o-tech embedded in the mask.

Before Soren even moves, vector lines appear in my line of sight, parsing out all potential moves he could make as I absorb the probabilities related to each one. My aura field is an evolving grid of actions and reactions blended into a reality that I must constantly interpret. All these details and numbers strike me like mini bolts of lightning, zipping through the tundra of my mind, and I see him then in our apartment—the day I lost both him and Dad.

The memory tightens my throat and I'm seeing glimpses of my final moments with them in quick decisive bursts of light: Soren's bloody fists, his hot rage, the snap of bone as he swings his lead pipe at the guard, Juror Harmeny, the glint of a needle as she drives it into Soren's neck in an arc, and me, yelling and pleading for my Dad, telling them he's too old and broken to work for the Crown. I was the one who stole. It was my idea, so take me instead!

I knew the survival rate of miners; I knew what imprisonment by the Crown meant.

Harmeny's warm voice instilled a hate in me that has never died. "But you are not the one with the rage. Don't worry, child—I have different plans for you."

All of it, the fierce light being sucked away from our home as they left me in darkness, the shouts from Soren, the blood—comes together in a whirling image.

Soren is a different person now. That day his rage was unbound and dangerous; today it will be turned against me.

Unless I do something about it.

The announcer's voice snaps me from my reverie. "Ladies and gentlemen, have we got a match for you. Welcome to the final round of the Fall Gauntlet—lynx versus bear!"

THREE

As the stadium erupts with cheers and shouts, all I can think about is how I've put everything into this moment.

I've trained with Master Gherus and learned everything I could about the 3-D nanoparticle projection capabilities of phosphotech, the algorithmic, raw computing power of ciantech and its embedded microchips, and my favorite, what I began to learn firsthand through mask integration—the fission elements and their ability to power o-tech and its endlessly complex mechanisms—so that I could one day be strong enough to fight in the gauntlet and bring my mother back with a single wish.

I've fought like an animal that knows each fight may be its last, and it was a choice I made willingly. I've been clobbered to the point of blacking out, beaten and bruised until my body was a black and blue balloon. I've ended a life with a gem staff blow to the head. I'm not just clever anymore with my technology and ability to make connections. I can see and guess beyond the present moment and have become a fighter, the fighter I've always wanted to be. I've made it past the grunt rounds where so many skilled fighters fall and die to become one of sixteen champions, then on to the finals, only to find out that perhaps combat and survival is in our family's blood.

My body is relaxed and at ease, falling into a quiet calm that overtakes me and allows instinct to drive. My mind is on the brink of utter disarray, fractured, communicating with my heart in weak, tampered signals, and all of me is about to come undone.

I hear D's voice in my head. "You have to pull out."

I can't think straight. I shouldn't be thinking at all because thinking gets you killed. "You have to just act," Master Gherus had said. "You have to let instinct guide you."

Is that what I'm supposed to do? Tap into the ever-flowing fountain of wisdom that I was graced with? It doesn't matter. Wisdom is irrelevant now.

I need to act and be one step ahead.

Our match begins. As I step onto the arena my thoughts show me the main component of our "floating" platform, held up by long chains attached to the four corners of the massive block of sandstone. I've always known it, but today my mask is showing me the camo tech that gives the crowd the visual enjoyment of a floating isle.

Across from where I stand, one hundred feet away, Soren steps onto the battle arena. My mask's aura field activates, and I ingest all the probabilities related to his potential actions. Each one carries more weight than I've ever known as the blue lines disperse, retract, then branch into new pathways all leading to one single outcome: Soren's death, or my own.

I don't know if the bear knows who he's fighting or not.

The vectors display a quick burst of micro movements that I've come to understand as certain emotions, so my guess is he doesn't. Based on his strong, decisive steps forward, my intuition tells me he'll have no qualms about killing me. I now know that Soren did not receive the same kind of information that I did.

That's where it gets complicated.

I need him to know who I am so that he doesn't kill me, but I'm also not allowed to remove my mask—one of the two gauntlet rules—so I'll need to tell him in words. Then comes our next dilemma: if neither of us wins, then it's a draw, which isn't technically against the rules, but there has to be a winner. The Crown will accept nothing less, and it's clear to me now that they've orchestrated this outcome. It's too perfect. Brother versus brother. They want to see this match play out just as much as our people do, but for different reasons—reasons I haven't yet figured out.

It doesn't matter though, because Soren is approaching me. His giant gauntlets with their metal claws gleam in the piercing autumn sun with every step as he grips a massive, spiked club that he could use to slaughter a whale.

I step forward to meet him but now the vectors are inverting and collapsing within the aura field, and I digest the minute probability that I will have to raise arms against Soren and strike him dead. The vision shows me striking him with the gem of my staff over and over, quick and merciless. I'm getting sick thinking about it. I can't do it, so I pull away from the vision. The Crown wants me to, but I can't. I'd save Mom upon victory, but something about this isn't right. Gracious goddess—nothing about this is right.

I don't have time to decide what is right, only to dodge Soren's first attack. He swings his massive club at me, once, twice, as I duck under the first and jump over the second. I start to swing my staff but can't gain momentum because he lunges at me again, his claw cutting through the air with enough velocity to slice me open. I intuit to see the odds of his movements, glimpsing and attaching to a deceleration of his latest jab, giving me enough time to sidestep away from him and into the captured insight. My guess is correct. He's open to attack, so I kick his inner thigh, once, twice, then rap my gem staff against the crook of his elbow. He groans, tries to shake it off, but he can't. I've hit a pressure point.

The bear's eyes are hell inside his mask, the skin around them pulsing violet. He isn't stunned anymore, so he swipes at me with his other hand.

"The bear does not hesitate, and yet he is!" the announcer says. The crowd takes in a collective breath, experiencing a minor bout of confusion as they realize that their chosen hero is not perfect.

Now that I'm close enough to see Soren's eyes, I feel more of him, my brother, his innocence ripped from him, all the rage he's held onto and has never released. Defeating me won't help. It never helps. I push down the beginnings of bile in my throat, my skin crawling at the thought of one of us dying today.

I need Soren to know it's me.

Stepping back and away with lithe movements and no clue of what I will do once Soren sees me—I'll probably be executed for breaking the rule, but it's better than having to murder my brother—I grab my mask under the chin and pull.

It won't budge. It's held in place as if by sap.

Soren is back, swinging. Above the crowd, his voice is clear, booming, no longer the voice of a young boy. "Your death is the fate of our people. Accept it."

It's one of the bear's incantations. The words strike me with more force than a club to the chest. I falter. He seizes the opening, grabbing me by the neck like I'm a slab of meat that he can squeeze the blood from.

I'm in Soren's death grip, and yet the Crown holds both of us in theirs. Breaking his stronghold on me is the first step in breaking their hold on my family and our nation.

"Soren!" I manage to say with a collapsing trachea.

His nostrils flare. He loosens his grip enough for me to steal a breath.

I throw my weight forward and kick up, my boot slamming against his skull. He releases me enough for me to land and back away toward the edge to catch my breath.

"How did you—" he says.

Before, all I saw was a bear hellbent on spilling blood, and now I see a hurt, injured human, fighting for something as well. I haven't had time to think about what Soren might wish for. Now, he's calculating who I am, how I know his name, how this lynx is able to say something in a voice so similar to the brother he once had.

Soren is not prepared for this truth hurtling towards him.

He cannot fathom that I could be here now.

The Crown has done something to my mask to make sure I can't remove it. They're one step ahead. They know that if either of us shows our faces, we'll drop our arms and refuse to fight. They broke Soren and turned him into their lapdog, but they cannot come between brothers. Not brothers like Soren and me.

I know more about the masks than the common champion since I had helped build some of the phospho-imaging tech in them. You can deactivate the masks, canceling out the image that they project onto the person, by tripping the sensors, which can be done by overheating them. Once deactivated, I'll also be able to remove it.

"The Crown said my opponent would try to trick me, the lynx especially."

The Crown has already gotten to him, and I'm wondering how deep the trust goes, but I have more pressing matters to worry about.

Soren bounds forward in a rage. I stand my ground. He swings his claw at me, which I dodge, but then he does exactly what I want him to do next—he sweeps his claw in a backhand motion. Turning ninety degrees so that my torso takes the brunt of the attack, I use the force of his swipe to launch myself onto the ground, making sure to keep the temple of my mask pressed to the platform. My entire body sings out in pain as I slide across the arena.

I lose track of time, of the sounds around me, and stagger to my feet. I'd underestimated Soren's power and now my torso is cut open and gushing blood. I grimace, holding the wound. It was my only option. I fall to one knee and feel around for the tiniest latch on the inside of the mask, which will release it from my face as long as the sensor has been tripped.

Soren is bounding forward again. The announcer is blathering on that my final moments have come. Not today.

I tear my mask from my face, and this time it comes off clean. The warm air sucks the breath out of my lungs. I've lost my powers of precognition, my staff is now heavier than I can hold, and it feels like I'm suddenly naked in a room full of strangers, devoid of even an ounce of power.

The entire stadium falls silent.

I've just broken a Fall Gauntlet rule, and everyone sees that I—Benji Calyx—am the lynx. I don't care. As long as Soren knows, I've accomplished my mission. If he still wants to kill me now, then there's nothing I can do to get him back.

The bear runs forward, ready to swing his club to knock my head clean off, but stops dead in his tracks. He's clocked who I am, like I am a ghost returned from the past.

His shoulders drop and his hands fall to his sides. He draws in a long breath, like his body cannot process this moment. The rage is still there, but there is something else too. He leans forward and I can smell his hot breath, sticky with the scent of rice and stale coffee.

"Benji?" he asks.

FOUR

Several moments pass before anyone reacts, and then—utter chaos. The stadium erupts into a cacophony of sound, as anger rips through the warmed air like a hurricane. People shout and throw garbage at the arena with betrayal in their hateful and confused cries, a betrayal of what people of the land have come to see on this final day of the tournament.

"The lynx has unmasked himself!" the announcer says. "Our masked marauder has revealed his true identity."

It doesn't matter. I don't care who knows me. Winning has become irrelevant. It would have saved my mother, but the Crown has turned it into something I could never live with.

"What . . . is this?" Soren asks. His eyes are like amber diamonds behind his well-crafted mask, and I sense the universe of sadness swirling inside them. "How did you—?" Soren turns with a sharp movement to look at the crowd, as though this is their fault. Maybe it is.

"Is the lynx playing some kind of mental game?" the announcer asks.

People in the stadium are booing us now, throwing wads of garbage. Objects pepper the intense sunlight like a random swarm of insects flying at us.

"Soren," I say while watching him, trying to anticipate what will come next, even without my mask. I think that I know him. I want to know him again, but the truth is, I don't know what he will do.

I run from the landslide of thoughts in my brain, trying not to be crushed by the weight of it. They can't force us to murder each other.

"We have to get out of here," I say. "Escape together. The Crown has been planning for us to meet like this for years." I don't know the truth of that statement, but the clues are coming together now, and they seem irrefutable. It's at least a seed for Soren to chew on, and that's a start. I don't know how to communicate with this brother that has been taken from me.

Everything happens fast after that. Our voices are drowned out by the people, some of them once loyal to the lynx, and some of them still loyal to the bear, who has not revealed his identity.

"What will the bear do now that the lynx is just a man?" the announcer asks.

Soren's grip tenses around his club. Inside his gauntlets, his hands tighten into fists. Maybe he's so far gone, brainwashed by the very people who've destroyed his life that he no longer knows me, and has no problem striking me down. But then he says, "How can we escape? The Crown is everywhere."

I've reached some part of him. He's questioning. He's always been curious, open-minded in ways that used to surprise me, interested in justice, curious about all angles. It is fitting that he is the bear, the totem with the ability to pass between the spirit realm and ours.

"Stand down," I say. "If you stand with me in solidarity they have to fight us both."

"They'll kill us," Soren says, but his voice exudes no fear. "I don't understand how you're here. They told me you were—" Soren's head drops a hair's breadth. He loosens his hold on his club, then as if to let everyone know where he stands in this fight, he releases hold of his gauntlets. They fall to the ground with a thud. His bare hands are even more menacing than the gauntlets twice their size.

The fight is over. For now. The announcer stalls and drones on about there never having been a match like this.

Don't I know it.

Metalmen are there the next instant, cuffing us and leading us back to our platforms, back down to the tunnels to return to our holding cells. I don't know what will come next, but I can guess.

"The Crown locked my mask," I tell D as soon as she visits me once I am back in my cell. She doesn't come with food like she usually does after a match, but then again, I haven't won.

"Benji, how did you break the code?" D asks. Her question is focused and informed, and there is something in her eyes that says she knew this would happen. How does she know that the masks have codes? It's not common knowledge, and I've never talked about my ciantech days, but then again, there is a lot about D that I don't know. In fact, now that I watch her moving the blonde hair out of her eyes, her emerald-green eyes piercing my soul like the talons of a dragon, I realize that I don't know much about D at all.

The lynx's greatest strength is being able to see all that is known and unknown.

Under the tutelage of Master Gherus, I learned to never trust or believe anyone, and now I'm wondering who or what to believe, if Soren was merely playing a part, or if the Crown is, again, two steps ahead. I decide not since they didn't anticipate me breaking the code to their mask mid-battle.

"I just did," I tell D. "I had to reveal myself to Soren."

"It may have bought you some time, but . . ."

I watch D, trying to intuit how she's come across select information. Part of me is tempted to put my mask back on so I can see even more, but too much of the neurosync can fry my neurons, so I decide against it.

D says, "If neither you nor Soren win in the next match, they're going to kill you both. Public execution."

"How do you know?"

"I heard the other guards talking."

I track her eye movements, trying to detect any sign of a lie. I find nothing. "So what am I supposed to do?" I see Master Gherus in my mind's eye, in our days of apprenticeship, me at my station, tinkering, him shuffling over to inspect my handiwork, asking why I attached a wire in such an unconventional way, or why I couldn't do things the way others had done it before me. I try to think of what he'd tell me to do. "Escape?" I ask D, as if she is a substitute for my wise teacher.

"Benji?" D says, and I can sense she has more to say.

I meet her eyes and see death in them, like she has seen it before and knows its shape and color. A darkness creeps across the horizon of her bright eyes. "What else did you hear, D?"

"It's about your dad."

A deep sigh leaves my body. I don't want the Crown pulling anyone else in my family into this ordeal, but I'm afraid my wishes mean nothing at this point.

"He had a wish too."

"Oh?"

"His wish was to save his own life. In exchange, he was tasked with moving the pieces that would set you and Soren against each other today."

My mouth falls open. I don't know what the truth is anymore—what is real and what the Crown has invented to destroy my family further. My throat tightens. I don't want to believe it. Who wants to believe that their father would betray them, give them away to the Crown dogs in exchange for his own life?

But then I remember my father and the last time I saw him when my mother was still with us. How he cowered and said nothing as they took her away. I try to separate what I want to believe and what is truth, but it's getting harder these days.

Now I realize what our family meant to the Crown, what we represented. I never learned enough about what Mom was planning to know the level of threat she presented. But I knew that Soren and I had not advanced to the final round of the gauntlet by chance. Even now, we would pay for the sins of our traitorous parents.

I have a plan, but I'm going to need some time.

"When do we go again?" I ask D.

She shakes her head as though the next match will be even worse than the first. "I don't know, but I'll find out."

D leaves my cell, and I wrack my brain for solutions to my problem, playing out every possible scenario now that Soren is an integral piece in this puzzle. What would Gherus tell me now? How would he approach this life-or-death anomaly? I turn back to my makeshift desk, a slab of stone built into the wall with a wooden stool underneath, the giant book of lore lying closed like a tome of secrets on top. Gherus would tell me that the Crown is not a complicated entity. They have power and control, but the clues as to how they will make their next move are all there.

Approaching my desk and staring at the rows of totems on the front of the book, I know there must be some answer for me inside. I open the heavy book to the lynx totem and start reading as I've done thousands of times. This time, I am looking for something different.

FIVE

My candle is flickering to its final flames by the time I look up from the totem lore. My eyes burn. The lynx lore I know by heart, but I had to reread parts about the bear. I haven't familiarized myself with the other totems because I thought it would distract me from my mission. Anything that doesn't help me win is a distraction. But this will help me win. Knowing that my final opponent is the bear and having a second chance to think about what the match means is a gift. One the Crown does not readily give. I know what they'll do next. One of us has to win, and if neither of us delivers the finishing blow, they'll force one of us to. After all this time, they have to have a champion. The nation depends on it. The question is, which one of us do they favor?

When D returns, I'm weary from reading, but the darkness I now find myself in is somehow soothing. D carries an oil light, and I see defeat in her eyes, as if she's been admonished since I'd last seen her hours before. "Your match is a week away," she says.

This is the norm between matches so that the champions can rest, but Soren and I haven't really fought or injured each other at all, so a week seems unnecessary. "A week? I can't wait a week."

"Benji, you can't believe anything I say," D says. Shadows dance across her face, and I can't fully read her expression.

"Should I believe that?" I know the Crown's tricks, and this might be of them.

"I'm serious," D says.

"Then why say anything at all?"

D hesitates. She's been roped into this tournament as my confidante and may have been chosen based on our compatibility. Our relationship has never been romantic for me, because I don't have time to think about that, but she grows softer each time she comes to visit me. She's no longer just the guard of my holding cell. She's invested in my success. "I keep overhearing things, and I think it's a setup. They want me to hear and tell you."

"To confuse me and throw me off course?"

"Maybe."

I grab at the fine hairs on my chin. "Keep telling me. I'll decide what's true or not. I am the lynx, after all. What did you hear this time?"

D sighs. "Your stunt of revealing your identity angered the Crown."

"No surprise there."

"The people know that you and Soren must have known each other. Now people are wondering if the gauntlet has always been about pitting loved ones against each other."

Are Soren and I the exception or the rule?

"You have to think about other champions that have won."

"Everyone knows the eagle won last time," I say.

"What happens to them after?" D asks.

"No one knows," I say.

D looks at me, her eyebrows raised. She waits.

"They don't live, do they?"

"Their wish may come true," D says. "They may live, but their lives are not theirs."

"So the Crown owns them."

"That's all I know," D says, releasing a sigh, as though holding those truths inside her was too much, and now she can breathe again.

I'm taking it all in as Mom, Soren, and Dad swim through my thoughts. What will happen to each of us? Will any of us ever be together again? Closing my eyes, I try to breathe and focus on the next match as I always have. I don't see how it's possible to get out of this alive. I can't have everything that I want. Saving Mom means killing Soren, but what does saving Soren and myself look like?

"Can you get a message to Soren, D?"

She shakes her head. "I don't know where he's being held. I think he's under the Crown's control, Benji."

I need help, but Soren is right—the Crown is everywhere, all knowing, ruling with their iron fist and steel blade. What can I do? The only powerful entities are the Crown or the totems.

"D, what shifts the tides of battle?" I need to talk out loud, move through this problem with someone else.

"It's hopeless, Benji. The Crown has thought of everything. If you shift the tides of battle, you win. If Soren does, he wins. His wish is to save your father."

"How do you know that?"

"I heard it, like everything else."

"So he may kill me."

"I don't think he has a choice."

"We always have a choice." The Crown wants me to strike him down. This information that D brings to me, true or not, is carrying me closer to my own truth. Out of the two of us, the Crown not only favors the totem whose lore will rescue the people, they favor the brother who is easier to manipulate.

The facts begin slamming into me like meteorites. Soren may be the Crown's lapdog, but they can't extinguish his rage. I saw it in his eyes. If he wants to, if he goes berserk again, he can murder whomever he wants. Under the tutelage of Gherus, I had been the Crown's dog too. I'd made them weapons and masks and new tech. I was the easier of the two brothers to control. I was the totem favored to win. My victory means four years of the sciences, something the Crown has always been hesitant to introduce to their people, but perhaps they need it now. Perhaps I am the answer.

But winning is playing right into their hand. I also have to get Soren out, and I'm beginning to get an idea.

"There is no power without the Crown," D says at last. "They're a black hole sucking in all light."

"The eagle effected change because the people believed and followed. What would the Crown be without its people following?"

D stares at me, and her eyes well up with a newfound misery. "And how do you expect to get the people to follow you and not the Crown?"

I think for a moment, recalling what I've just read about the lynx and the bear. There are so many tiny details that could carry weight if executed correctly. "Okay. Soren is out, but there's someone else I need you to get a message to."

"I have a feeling the Crown will be watching what I do," D says.

"Then you'll have to be careful. Sounds like we have plenty of time."

SIX

There are some things more painful than death. Not that I've died before. The week before my second matchup against Soren was torture. Every morning, D would come to me with more news, and I was beginning to think that I shouldn't believe anything she said. That everything she heard was part of some larger plan to unhinge me. The Crown is no stranger to psychological torment, and based on what I was hearing, I was worried about what they were feeding to Soren.

I've become mentally tough because I had Gherus's support and I've adopted healthy coping strategies, but I don't know if Soren ever has. His coping strategies come from anger, from kicking guards and breaking their bones, which is what got him taken away in the first place.

By the time I enter the stadium, I've detached myself from all information. All that matters is what I'm going to do. I can't make any mistakes today. A single one could cost me my life, or Soren's.

I couldn't reach him during our week of solitude, so I had to rely on our brotherhood, our shared love for each other and our family, for my plan to work. Cold, brilliant sunlight tickles my exposed skin when my platform reaches the arena. Soren stands across from me, and I see the depth of his bear persona. His mask is menacing with its round, knowing eyes, bared teeth, pointed ears, and coarse hair covering the cheeks. The veins in his arms bulge, almost reptilian. His muscles are twice as big as mine.

"Ladies and gentlemen, we return for the final match of our Fall Gauntlet," the announcer says, his voice profound and perfect with the help of the voice amplifier. The air is crisp, colder than it was a week ago as our planet enters the autumn season. "The lynx will face off against the bear, and there shall be only one victor."

Soren and I step onto the arena in sync, and I try to intuit what he might be thinking. If his wish is truly to save Dad, I wonder who—if this is an accurate litmus test—he loves more. Perhaps he's had contact with Dad over the years or has been made to believe that he is close to saving him. There is something in the way he stands, with his chin tucked to his chest, revealing no neck, no sign of weakness, that makes me question everything about this past week and my own plan.

Would he really kill me to save Dad?

The time for thinking is over. I fumble with the voice piece in my pocket, the final gift given to me by D mere hours before the match. If science and knowledge are the way of the lynx, then I shall use my voice to challenge the Crown's. All I need is for Soren to sit still long enough to not attack me while I deliver my message.

It doesn't happen quite like that.

As soon as I pull out the voice piece, Soren is on me. He barrels forward as though on his paws, then swipes at me, claws out and sharpened. I back away, clutching my voice piece, tucking it back into my pants where it will be safe.

"Soren! You have to work with me!"

He stands tall, then lunges at me with all his weight forward. I'm near the edge, and could, with the appropriate footwork, invade his center of gravity and put him in a compromised position: off-balance, momentum racing forward to the point that I could send him careening off the edge. But I can't.

Instead, I sidestep, then dance around his jabs, just out of range, scanning his eyes, where his mind might be. He doesn't respond to me, doesn't even acknowledge that I've said anything, and now he's given himself away.

"The bear will do anything to protect its people," the announcer says. "He knows the winter will be hard, and he will be the protector."

Soren is in a mild state of his signature berserk mode, and I know that his mission—whether he's chosen this himself or not—is to end me, which in turn will push me to end him, thus playing right into the Crown's plan. Now I'm sure of it. I've seen the look in his eyes, the same look he had when they took Dad away. The Crown has commandeered his behavior, and I need to do exactly as Harmeny did that day and knock him out. But only for a minute. I need him to walk out of here on his own two feet with me.

He's at the edge now, and I have the advantage.

I swing my staff at his neck, which he's still protecting. He swipes those wild and massive claws at me, and I feel the rush of wind against my chest and my torso as he moves again and again against me. It becomes a flurry of swings and swipes, the staff of science and knowledge versus paws of grit and might. When they clash, there are sparks of light, glinting off the metal blades in his claws as they collide with the rhodamium in my staff's gemstone.

The people are shouting and cheering.

I've lost some muscle definition during the week, spending more time on reading than on push-ups and planks, and Soren seems to have doubled in strength, like he's been eating all week. He's full, near bloated, his muscles holding maximum water, and I've leaned out even more. It's not always about strength, though. Sometimes it's about precision. Getting the right message to the right people at the right time.

Or striking when there is an opening.

Soren leaves one as he swipes in a backhand motion, his temple exposed. I step on his arm to launch myself high into the air, pull my staff back behind my shoulder, then drive it at his temple. The mask cracks. I land and back away, making sure to put plenty of distance between us. He's in berserk mode because of the mask, and now I've cracked whatever code had him in his straitjacket of servitude.

He staggers backward, tries to readjust his mask, but I'm already speaking into the voice piece.

"People of New Phasia!" My voice is hoarse. I'm not used to addressing this many people at once, but the amplifier carries it well enough.

The shouts of the crowd go from sheer anger and rage to mild confusion, as though their hopes and fears have been dampened by sudden rain. I know the announcer wants to speak, but he has never seen anything like this, and he's trying to see how it will go. What he'll need to do to control the situation. He's not nobody. With the power of voice in my hands now, I know that he stands for the Crown's power today and throughout the tournament. Whoever can get the message across holds the power.

"The lynx thinks he can whisper words to you so that he doesn't have to fight," the announcer says.

I'm prepared for this tactic and bend it to my own plan. "And the Crown wants my brother, Soren—the bear—and I to fight, so that they never have to. When you think of the Crown, who do you see?"

The crowd has fallen silent. Only the soft wisp of wind blowing through the arena can be heard. The sounds of trumpets and drums have died out. It is so quiet that my voice echoes for a moment through the stadium. The vector field in my line of sight is exploding into a wild amalgamation of probabilities and ratios that are too overwhelming to parse out. I press on.

"You don't see anyone because the Crown is the ultimate coward. Their faces are our"— and I point to my mask and then to Soren—"our faces. And for as long as you live, this is how it will always be. Fighter versus fighter. Loved one versus loved one. Fighting to the death so that they can exact upon their people whatever new prophecy will fit their agenda, year after year. Well, I ask you, my people—my lynx and my bears, not one or the other—I ask all of you, brothers and sisters, who will truly have your back in the end: your own flesh and blood, or the Crown?"

"The lynx has gone a little crazy," the announcer says. "He's spent too much time in his tunnels, don't you think?"

The crowd remains silent.

"So I ask you in these final moments where the Crown has asked you to play witness to brothers who have been pitted against each other over the past seven years, who have been separated from each other, each made to believe that the other is dead, one brainwashed to believe that saving his mother is the only way forward, and the other made to believe that saving his father is the only way forward. People of New Phasia, if you have a loved one out there serving the Crown, or secretly groomed to fight in the next Fall Gauntlet, then ask yourself: What else have you got to lose? I know there are those out there who would choose the people—not the lynx or the bear, but both—as a new reality and way forward. The old way of one champion and four years of Harvest will not yield anything new. The only way to change our lives moving forward is to break this pattern and stand up against the Crown. To stand up with me and my brother!"

I fall silent, trying to catch my breath, blacking out some of these last moments, as my mind tries to comprehend what I am doing, this tactical interruption that will be my death or my life.

Now's the time.

Soren is adjusting his mask, regaining his balance, his brainwashed thoughts and feelings fed to him by way of the mask now in question.

"If you are with me, then fight with me. End the voice of the Crown and their tyranny by overtaking the announcer's box. Father of the lynx and mother of the bear, show yourselves and do what you have always wanted to do."

My final message must have gotten to an old friend of mine, because the supposed standing leaders of the lynx and the bear make moves to storm the announcer's box.

Everything happens so fast.

I've gotten my messages across, and the wave that will become the first riot in the history of the Fall Gauntlet begins as a curtain moving and falling upon us. Dark clouds storm overhead, and droplets of rain fall on my head, cooling my skin. Will the Dei see what I'm doing and interfere? Soren lunges for me again, but I sidestep and hit the crack that I've already created in his mask, making it bigger. It connects and his mask falls to the ground with a thud.

"Soren, you have to come with me!"

I know he's been brainwashed because when he looks at me, his eyes wide and bewildered, shaking off the power that has been controlling him, he seems ready to break.

"Benji?" It's like he's seeing me again for the first time. The Crown has done something to his memory. "What . . . is this?" He wants to break down and cry, but I can't let him.

"We're going now, Soren. Follow me!"

He's lost a part of his mind, but the part that is still there sees that his brother has come back to save him.

I run to the arena's corner and as if on cue, the chains that hold up the platform appear, materializing out of thin air, the camo tech disabling, allowing us to see their true form. They connect to the platform's corners and then run up and over the stands to giant pillars behind the stadium. The chains are wide and sturdy—not the perfect escape route, but better than what is below. I step onto the chain and look behind me at Soren's dazed expression. His skin is pale, ghastly even, like this choice of escape is worse than death.

"Follow me, Soren. Hold onto me if you need to."

"What are we doing?" Soren yells at me, his voice gruff and gravelly from disuse.

"We're going to save Mom and Dad. And we're going to do it our way."

Soren says nothing, just stares at me wide-eyed, as though he's not sure if I'm someone he can trust yet, this brother that he hasn't seen in so long. But the promise of saving Dad may be enough for him to trust me for now.

His giant bear claw touches my gauntlet, and we hold each other in place. As a feline totem, balance has never been a problem for me. Soren couldn't do this alone, not now, I know, but he's with me.

"But the Crown," Soren says. "They'll find us. Kill us."

"Doesn't seem any different than any other day," I say, starting to scale the chains, leading Soren along. "Let them try. I'm not leaving you again."

SEVEN

The day the Crown took Mom away was a dark one for our family, but it wasn't until they took Dad and Soren that life really changed. For years I secretly tried to find out what happened to Mom. Since she was named a traitor, it would have been dangerous to talk or ask about her openly. When Dad and Soren left, I knew what happened to them, but somehow they seemed more distant than Mom. Maybe they died in my mind that day because I knew the Crown controlled them. With Mom, I always believed she'd be fighting back in her own way.

The guard who took her away said that Mom was going to an off-world prison. I knew that there were other planets and galaxies in the great beyond, but I had no knowledge of what they were or where they might be. I had no knowledge of any ships or spacecraft that we had on Calypso, but then again, I had no knowledge of the tech the Crown was using until I was inside the castle walls making some of it myself.

The day Dad and Soren were taken, I spent the entire night thinking of what I could do to get Mom back. I spent that first night alone, in a paralyzed, blind rage, my thoughts rushing through the twisted labyrinth of my mind. Later, I learned that I was experiencing a new kind of trauma, compounding and more powerful than the first, which was causing my brain to stretch and grow in new ways. There were fires burning new neural networks and pathways, so of course, I did not sleep.

When Harmeny returned the next day, her eyes twinkling with an insatiable hunger for new lives she could undo, I went willingly to my trial, because what else could I do? I was a different boy, hardened by the long, cruel night and the repeated images of Soren and his wild eyes, the lead pipe slashing through the air, glinting like a beastly claw, and then the sickening snap of bone. Haunted by the images of Dad hobbling off, his own ruined leg forever on the verge of healing just enough to only be broken but destabilized by perpetual infection. The medicine we'd stolen was intended to save his life, for we knew very little about the lifecycles of bacteria and infection at our ripe ages of ten and eight.

I stood trial for my crimes, for orchestrating a heist from a clinic, breaking and entering, accomplice to assault and battery, and a long list of other irrefutable grievances. My sentence was not the mines like Soren, who'd need to temper his anger, and what better place than the claustrophobic, soul-crushing darkness of the underground? My sentence was not the servitude that my father would face, although I did not know what happened to him at the time. No, my sentence would be one of science, in service to the Crown. Harmeny had seen my talents—she often congratulated herself for being a people person—with the gripclaw she'd learned had helped me climb during my days as a thief. She saw that I had potential in making things. Even things the Crown had not yet made.

When I'd learned about the Fall Gauntlet, about the wish granted to champions, about Harvest and the four-year cycles that each totem initiated upon victory, I began bending my studies to my own will. I learned as much as I could from Gherus during our time together and created weapons and devices for the Crown without error. I also began to learn things for myself.

And now, as Soren and I tread on the now-visible chains that will be our escape out of the stadium, I know I will need to learn many more things. Like how to run and escape from a ruling body that would have our heads for breaking the totem cycle and starting a revolution.

The crowd's screams reverberate in my ears as I try to lead Soren higher on the chain. His careful steps are not cat-like, nimble, and lithe like mine, but more rooted to things of the ground. Still, he's making it okay, just like he did when we'd scale buildings. It would take him longer than me, but he'd always get there.

The shouts encircling us are warlike. Battle cries balloon and collapse within the arena as though we are in a bubble. I do not know if people are dying or if this is more of a demonstration of strength, a symbol of what the bears and lynx can do if they team up and fight back.

Sweat pours down my forehead and arms. I still wear my mask, but Soren does not. Those looking close enough could see the resemblance: the round, full face and angular jaw, the same dark hair, cut short, the same determined look in our light eyes—mine sea blue, his amber—thirsty to bring back those taken from us.

It is the look of a survivor, a pained warrior, a maker of change.

We're at the stadium's upper lip before I know it. The gauntlet arena looks clean and inviting from here, the demarcation lines on the battle platform black and neat. So many battles fought, so many useless deaths. Could I have done anything differently?

I step off the chain and onto the stadium wall wide enough for half my foot. I pull Soren to me in a great sweep as I sidestep to give him room. Grabbing his bicep, I hold his giant frame in place, steadying us both. He's still shaky, still unsure of these jarring changes in the course of his history.

"Soren!" I shout above the barrage of noise below me and all around. "We need to leave the city. The South Gate is closest, so we'll pass through there. We need to move. They'll be locking us in soon if they haven't already. Are you ready for this?"

The hesitation in Soren's eyes is a universe all its own. His pupils are dilating like crazy, taking in new light, and I sense the slightest shake in his body, like he used to do when he slept. He breathes deep through his nose, and his chest rises and falls like the cataclysmic shifting of tectonic plates. He knows his next move will send shockwaves through our lives. He does not use words, only nods his large head, and I know it's time to run like hell.

We find chains on the back wall and scale down, like we did when we stole for Dad.

On the ground, the gates are already closed like I thought they might be, but they're accompanied by chaos. People are running through the labyrinth of streets, a crisscross of movement, some of them retreating, cowering in fear, others with stolen goods or handheld blades or shields.

When we stop to catch our breath after five minutes of running without stopping, I feel a sense of victory—though I know it is small and only the beginning of our struggles—wash over me. It fills me with such gusto that I don't know how to contain it or process it. This is the first time I've stood up to the Crown, and right now, it feels like we have the upper hand. My whole body tingles. I'm not even worried about the five metalmen that stand between us and the gate.

"Benji?" Soren says, his breaths a wheezing rasp. He's not used to this kind of running. "Now what?"

I cannot fight the grin that finds its way onto my face.

"Stand down," one of the metalmen says, and all at once, the entourage points their broad blades at us, dropping one foot back to assume battle stance. "All lynx imposters and sympathizers are under arrest and will face judgment."

A laugh escapes me. Soren is still looking at me for what to do, so I say, "I think we've faced enough judgment for a lifetime." I readjust my gem staff in my hand. If they don't know the identity of the person behind the mask, they soon will. They cannot see my elation as I turn to Soren. "What do you say we knock some heads one last time on our way out of town, bro?"

Soren flashes me the widest grin I have ever seen. "I thought you'd never ask."

END OF BOOK ONE

THE FALL GAUNTLET:

RAT

BOOK TWO

This book is dedicated to anyone who wears a scar left by family. It is this pain that makes you precisely who you are.

RAT

It is said that the rat was not seen on Calypso for many millennia; some even believed it had gone extinct, crushed underfoot by any creature that walked its path.

Would it be unreasonable to think that not every first animal wanted to be seen? That perhaps not every creature walks in the light with brawn and might?

Totem scholars believe that the rat was one of the last Originals to leave the planet, that it had been watching from the shadows, waiting for a human champion to call its name and bring evolution to all living things.

When the rat's shadow passes on the wall at your feet, listen to its tiny, purposeful steps. Smell the fear it lives with every day. Learn how it turns the world on its axis to its advantage.

That is when the rat will act.
That is when the rat becomes you.

The Book of Totems, Rat

ONE

S oren and I knock out the metalmen standing between us and freedom, and we flee like animals from a thunderstorm, frantic and determined to find safety. In those early moments of escape from the Fall Gauntlet and the Crown itself, it's all we can do. The iron-toed boots of so many youthguard clattering across the cobblestones toward us is a warning song for the judgment that awaits us. Soren and I will pay for escaping the Fall Gauntlet together, not murdering each other, and therefore, not giving the Crown a champion. But we've been paying all our lives for the sins of our parents—why would now be any different?

Marketplaces I've frequented whiz by in my periphery as we sprint through another narrow street. I'm not exactly sure where we are going, but I know these cramped streets well enough from my time apprenticing under Master Gherus to get us to the edge of town by nightfall.

Not that I'm about to stop and ask for directions.

For the first time ever, New Phasia looks beautiful to me in the afternoon light of that first fateful day. A cacophony of chaotic noises rings through the capital as people shriek, swords and shields clash in combat, and fireworks paint the gray, clouded sky with bursting strokes of magenta and cyan blue—colors representing both the lynx and the bear, and the revolution that we've started.

The stunt I pulled back in the gauntlet, calling upon the bear and lynx totem leaders to start a riot, would have its consequences.

More of the capital's metalmen follow us, emerging from bustling alleys and striding down steps to greet us in battle wearing their old-fashioned breastplates. Soren seems distracted as he strikes them down, one after another, as though breaking porcelain pots for a prize. His spiked club connects with flesh and fresh blood spritzes my face like the first drops of rain. Soren looks around, sniffing the air.

"Soren, we have to go!" I grab his massive, gauntleted hand, yanking him toward me, and we sprint down another branching path.

"I can't leave," Soren says, his breathing heavy and his face flecked with blood. His broken bear mask is off. "Not yet," he says.

"Because of Dad?" I ask.

"No," he says. "We have to go back for my girlfriend."

"Girlfriend?" If I'm expecting Soren to say anything, 'girlfriend' is my last guess on the list. I still don't know my brother at all.

We're both exhausted, hungry, and sleep-deprived, and now we have romance to deal with? I look at the lumbering beast that is my brother and try to make peace with the fact that he is no longer an innocent eight-year-old boy. So much can change in seven years.

"Where is she?" I ask as we choose a new direction and bound down a set of stairs, then up another. My own lynx mask feels heavy on my face. The o-tech, the organix integrating with my own physiology, shows me new probabilities of our very near future. My mask's aura field expands, and vector lines elongate then constrict to suggest actions to take. In the gauntlet, an opponent's possible actions are limited and finite, but out here it's a different game. There are many more enemies, probabilities, and random variables—the sheer volume of potentials is new to me.

I focus my mental energy on how to exit the city. The truth is, I don't know. I'd have worn my mask longer to calculate our best path forward, but an intense pressure was building in my temples, like stillworms burrowing into me. Ripping my mask off, I brace myself for the transition back to normalcy as my dopamine, testosterone, and hundreds of other biometrics level out. An icy autumn wind grips me as the world swirls around me in a dizzying rush of clay and brickstone before stabilizing.

Soren grips my shoulders and squares me up to him, his amber eyes blazing. "I don't know where she lives, but I know where we could find her."

We stand at a literal crossroads.

More metalmen find us and swarm us like fireflies to light. We have to move, or New Phasia will become our tomb.

"Clear a path, Soren!"

My brother is becoming quite the great listener and ally. He ploughs through another round of metalmen, pushing us to an even narrower alleyway, then we run until my legs ache. Adrenaline pumps through my body, but my senses are slowing, dulling out, like a blade struck to stone one too many times. So many thoughts and feelings overtake my being during those early moments of escape, and it's impossible to think of everything.

When Soren and I emerge from another long stretch of alleyway into a courtyard, we find ourselves surrounded by apartment buildings on all sides. Through the opened windows above, I glimpse red drapes, golden trim, a jet-black piano as big as a bear.

"We're not in the slums anymore," Soren says.

The clouds eclipse the sun, and a chilling darkness envelopes my body.

Spiked gates shoot up from the ground behind us to our left and right, cutting off all three exits. I watch the gates reach twenty-five feet before stopping with a thud, and that's when I see our next round of opponents.

I know them as cirque-de-freaks—acrobats, trapeze artists, and illusionists—the capital's version of jesters, except these guys do not bring laughter. Their faces are painted in the cirque-de way: red blush on their cheeks, white paint, and long eyelashes adorning their faces. With their baggy, oversized clothing and short haircuts, it's difficult to identify their genders.

"Soren. They don't fight like the metalmen." I'd seen them protect nobles like personal bodyguards. "Don't underestimate them."

"Who are they?" I hear a tinge of fear in Soren's voice.

"Freakies," I say. "Super agile and quick. They'll bring you down through pressure points on your body. Do not let them get close to you. Don't let them touch your skin!"

The four newcomers drop down from the walls and gate like night itself, falling like a curtain. They sink into the shadow as though it's part of their uniform. I see little difference between them other than height.

They come at us in a flurry, and I hold my staff out in a defensive stance to keep them at bay. I hear and feel one of them behind me, so I duck, hold my gem staff near its end and swing back toward the movement. I miss, and the freakies are upon me, jabbing with fists of lightning.

"Soren, back-to-back!"

Soren's labored breathing and growing body heat are familiar, like a magnet drawing me in and calming my erratic nerves. Our backs touch. He's not yet panicked, but my heart is galloping in my chest in spite of his presence. The freakies are becoming difficult to track as they swing and fly through the night sky like monkey-bats. We swing and swing until it feels like they aren't even trying to fight, only tire us out.

Soren knows their tactics and breaks their pattern by charging at them as one of the freaks lands, and I have to hand it to him—he times it perfectly, like a flyswatter landing a millisecond after the fly does. Wind leaves the freak's body, and I hear bone crack at the ribs as it blasts into the wall. The other freakies lunge at Soren. I swing my staff at them, connect with one, and hear the freak reel in pain as I blast into their thigh muscle.

We've fought so many Fall Gauntlet rounds. I can't let myself lose to a couple of clowns, but I also know we can't go on like this. I hear metal grating against stone and have a sinking feeling that the gates locking us in are lowering, and someone more powerful is here to lock us up. Then I notice the sewer drain cover sliding open in front of me, and a man's small, bald head poking through.

"Down here," he says. "Those freakies won't follow, trust me. It'll get their dresses too dirty."

I do not want to, in any way, go into the sewers. I do not want to trust this strange man. I do not want to retreat into the darkness of the sewer, but the bald man keeps saying the right things.

"If you're trying to get out of the city, I can show you the way."

I grab Soren while I can, waiting for the man to move out of the way as I peer into the darkness.

"Jump," he says. "You'll be fine."

So we do.

The man slides the sewer lid closed above us, entombing us in a black abyss.

TWO

The sound of steady, coursing water greets us in the darkened sewers once we can hear more than just our own heaving breaths. I follow the sound of Soren's cursing and huffing and move closer. Heat rolls off his body in waves as he walks ahead of me.

The urge to put on my mask tugs at me, on neurons that are starved for its power, but I fight it, breathing in and out. Down here, the world is gray and endless, the capital's version of invented night.

The man's voice greets us again. "This way. Watch your step. There's a lot of trash down here."

"How are we supposed to see anything down here?" I ask.

"Follow the sound of my voice," the man says. "You'll only fall in if you're not careful. Listen to the water. It's not as hard as it seems."

Our new friend is right. The path lies straight ahead of us, the water to our right. We catch our labored breaths after a few minutes, and I realize how thick the air is with moisture, how this entire place lacks any sort of effective ventilation.

"How much further until we get out of here?" I ask.

"Depends on where you're going," the man says. "The sewers have a few exits out of the city. So, where are you fellas heading?"

It's strange to me that people choose to live in the sewers, but our mysterious savior seems content as he leads us onward—happy, even. Does he have any investment in the lynx versus bear finals, or even know about it? Beyond escaping the capital, I don't know where we are going. I've put all my energy into escaping the gauntlet, not what comes after.

"Dad has some brothers in the western province of—" I try to recall, but it's been so long since he's mentioned his brothers, so long since I've had a conversation with Dad, if that's what it could even be called. "We'll head west," I say, finally.

"An hour tops," the man says. "To get you fellas out of here."

What will happen to Mom and Dad now that we've fled the final fight without either of our wishes granted? Based on information inside *The Book of Totems*, I know this altered course will have implications.

A lamplight gives shape to Soren, and now as we turn a corner, I can see much more. Like a shapeshifting monster that can triple its size, the sewers open up in that moment to reveal a different beast: a vast and well-lit galaxy peppered with long, stark pockets of cement, stone, and iron bars cloaked in shadow.

Light streams down into the cavernous opening and gives the area a tranquil blue glow. The canals flanking the perimeter and inner walkways flow to other tunnels of the underground labyrinth. Water shimmers and reflects prisms of light onto the wall, and for the first time in a long time, I feel something like peace. If the sewer didn't smell like the capital's rotting insides, it might be nice. I sense the presence of unreleased gases, of phosphorus and sulfur, like so many experiments gone wrong.

We stop and look around. Soren seems disturbed by something, and a moment later, I see it too. People are sitting or lying down in dark crevices where the light can't reach. Dirt and grime sullies their exposed skin in muddy streaks, and their clothes are tattered. Their bones poke out like they are all elbows and knees. One of them ventures out of his dark enclosure, his teeth an abominable black.

"Who are you people?" I ask. "Why are you down here?"

Our new friend steps into the light, which gives more detail to his small face. His long, bulbous nose and large ears make his face look even smaller. When he smiles, his teeth are surprisingly neat and cared for. His voice and face make him look youthful, but I guess him to be in his forties. He continues to grin without answering my question.

One man joins us. "Who are these gentlemen?" His voice is stronger than his frail body suggests.

"I think they were just about to tell us," the small man says.

Soren and I exchange a long, knowing glance. "Brothers with no place else to go," I say. "There's nothing left for us in the capital."

"I know that one," says the newcomer.

"Say, is that them brothers fighting each other in the gauntlet? Look at that one's mask." A woman skulks up and pulls out wisps of her thinning hair.

"Could be," the small man says. "They could be part of the lynx and bear alliance. Everyone is wearing those masks now." He looks us up and down, at the masks on our sides, which we had neglected to hide. "Though not everyone with those masks look like these guys." He must sense our discomfort because he follows by saying, "Their business is their own. They don't have to tell us who they are if they don't want to."

"Good. Great," Soren says. "Now, which way out of here?"

"Right," the man says. "I know this may not be the most appealing spot for you boys, but it's home for us. Two big strapping men like you could really help us around here."

"Sorry, pops," Soren says. "We can't spend our days down here like dying rats."

As soon as Soren says it, I wish he hadn't. The man's eyes flicker in the darkness.

"He just associates rats with sewers," I say. "He didn't mean anything by it."

"Sure, no worries," the man says, but I can sense him holding back some emotion as he clenches his jaw. "We get that a lot. We are rats, but we're not dying. Surprised you haven't heard of us."

"Heard of you?" I ask, trying to hide my stupefaction.

"The Crown calls us the Rats, and they badly want us to die, but they can't seem to get rid of us all." The man beams. "We tussle with them every now and again, don't we guys?"

The other man nods, and the woman seems to straighten her back at this. A violin plays somewhere deeper in the sewers and the melancholic melody is somehow soothing. I haven't heard real music in so long, and the effect on me is profound. Our companions notice.

"A lot goes on down here that the capital doesn't know about."

"What exactly are you trying to do?" Even though Soren has offended them, I wonder if these sewer people can be allies. We have to win Mom and Dad back, and I know we need all the help we can get.

"Bring the bastards down," the man says. "We have a plan but it's going to take a bit more time to come to fruition. Like I said, you boys would be instrumental in helping us."

"Maybe another time," Soren says. "We gotta save my girlfriend first. Remember, Benji? We can go west after that. Which way would bring us back to the—uh—the gauntlet stadium?"

"Soren, we can't," I say, my voice firm. "We have to come back for her. Right now, we have to move."

Soren stares at me with cold amber eyes, this last fight inside him dying to embers. "You promise? Once things die down?"

"I promise." I give Soren a reassuring nod, then turn to our help out of here. "Which way, kind sir? We've already wasted too much time."

"Follow the sound of the violin," the man says. "That will take you to the Western Gate. Find the violinist, and she'll be able to point your way out." The man nods, and his eyes are kind then.

We thank him for his help and leave the epicenter of the sewer, following the music, this latest song of misery.

THREE

"Where were they keeping you during the tournament?" I ask Soren once we're alone again. Soren seems to sense where the music is coming from even without his mask's enhancements. Despite every path appearing identical and like a long, dingy hallway without any real exit, Soren is confident in our direction. "In the dungeons," he says. "You?"

"I was underneath the stadium. Dungeons? Is that the same thing?"

Soren leads us deeper through the sewers. Having worked in the mines, navigating dark spaces comes easier to him. "Don't think so. I was being held at the castle."

My stomach clenches, as though ready to take a punch. I want to ask Soren if he was the Crown's lapdog, but I'm afraid of the answer. I'm afraid to know Soren's wish, even, because admitting that he chose Dad over Mom means admitting that he hadn't chosen me. I shake those dark thoughts from my head and follow Soren deeper.

"Tell me about your girlfriend," I say.

"Her name is Abbi. I met her at the mines," Soren says, his voice heavy with years of untold pain.

The violin plays on like a mourning child, somber and desperate, and I know we're getting closer. Prisms of light filter in from storm drains and flicker on the walls, making it feel like we're walking through the arches of a dark reverse rainbow.

"I worked with her dad." Soren says.

"When did you leave the mines and start training for the gauntlet?" I ask.

Soren stops and turns to look at me. At first, I think my question has triggered an unpleasant memory, but I realize he's peering past me to our next set of branched paths. Our gazes meet and hold for a long moment. We are brothers finally able to look into each other's eyes again.

I see the span of his hurt running through the black and infinite abyss of his pupils, and he likely sees mine coursing like an endless loop of river doubling back on itself. I have the urge to hold him, scared that I may never get to again, but I'm too slow—Soren beats me to it.

He grabs me and forces our bodies together, our broken but healing hearts thumping against each other's chests. We speak no words, but I'm glad to be held by the younger brother I've always held and protected.

Until I couldn't.

Words of apology want to escape my throat then, but we stand apart, Soren holding me out like an intriguing old diary he doesn't want to open—both of us strong and whole, and yet full of broken pieces we're too afraid to show. After a long moment, we both look away, back to the mission at hand.

"I hear the violin this way," he says. "C'mon." We walk alongside the streams of water before Soren answers my question. "When I saved Abbi's dad. That's when the Crown decided to take me out of the mines."

"Why then?" I hate the Crown and don't want to talk about them, but they're an entity I need to understand. So many lives depend on it.

"I don't know," Soren says. "Probably something to do with my strength."

"What happened after that? You went straight to the dungeons?"

"No," Soren says. "I apprenticed under Master K.O."

"Master Kay Oh?" I ask.

"He made weapons for the Crown and needed an apprentice. Together, we made weapons twice as fast."

We were both assigned to weapon-making masters.

Soren stops walking and lifts his chin, searching for clues above ground. "There's a way out up there," he says, pointing to a drain above us.

I hear it too. The slow and clumsy shuffle of feet. The dying day turning to night. Shopkeepers take down their awnings, while others set up for the night bazaar, thrilled to sell rare trinkets or relics that supposedly come from another world. Part of me misses the superstition of our people, how they believe in totem animals that most of them have never seen before—not the Originals anyway, the first animals borne out of the sky, land, and sea—only the totems based on those legendary beasts, represented by strangers wearing masks.

"We haven't reached the violinist yet," I say. "It doesn't sound much farther."

"I don't want to trust that guy," Soren says. "What if the violin is another trap?" He pulls his mask out from his belt's holder and examines it. A crack carves a line at the mask's temple like a scar.

"The Rats"—I pause, wanting to admonish Soren for his earlier comment, but then think better of it—"they're fighting against the Crown too."

Soren holds my gaze. "I won't be able to fight like I used to," he says.

I wonder how much his mask changes his strength, sight, and ability. I've seen him fight against the freakies. He's still gauntlet champion material, but nine times out of ten he'd lose to me in a fight if I had my mask and he didn't.

"Let's find the violin. We don't know what's up there," I say.

"You sure, Benji?"

I hear my little brother's innocent voice in our apartment at that moment, but I'm looking upon a bear of a man. I shake those contrasting visuals from my mind and nod. "Follow me."

Soren does. Maybe he doesn't have the energy to argue or maybe he realizes I'm right. We trek forward through the tunnels as lights glimmer and the stench of trapped and rotting garbage grows, and in my own fatigue, the creeping thought that maybe Soren is right also grows. Are we walking into a trap? I'm not sure until I glimpse the silhouettes of a group up ahead. Soren curses. Instinct drives me to put my mask on as I hear the unsheathing of blades.

Joykillers.

A name used to encapsulate both the broadswords and the agents who wield them. Joykillers' plates are an inch thicker than the chainmail of youthguard, yet still sleek, with curved edges at the shoulders and knees, making them look a cross between the lithe youthguards and the experienced metalmen. Joykillers are true killers, assigned to the inner district close to the Crown. I've seen them before, but they always lurk in the shadows, the empire's final trump card.

They move at us with insane speed. I'm only able to react and divert the attacker's blade away from Soren's neck because the microhairs on my mask's ears alert me to danger. Instantly, I'm in gauntlet mode again as Soren's attacker slashes across his body, misses, then lunges for me. The only sound that echoes in the sewers then is the clash of sword on spiked club and the crack of staff at every weak point I can find, which is close to nothing. The second joykiller emerges from the other crossroad, barreling at me to take me two-on-one.

"Soren!" I call. "Go for the face!"

A joykiller's weakness is the tightness of their armor. One bash to the face and it can close on and collapse the structures necessary for life. A deviated septum or broken nose would never kill one of these bastards, but it can hinder them. And that's a start.

"How'd they find us?" Soren asks. He rips the air open with a sudden sweep of his club. The sound whistles in my ear.

The joykillers have been sent to end us, and I know it isn't coincidence that they find us here now.

That rat man. Soren offended him. I saw the look in his eyes, the look of shame and wanting to kill something that thinks it's better or bigger than you. He informed on us. Maybe for a reward.

My stomach tightens as I dodge the broadsword swings aimed at my head.

I fight like this for several minutes, only dodging, trying to stall enough for Soren to go for their faces, but their reaction time is ridiculous. Still, they aren't invincible. They exhale through the nose openings in their helmets, the first sound and sign that they are human, and square up with us.

This next round will be even more difficult, and I nudge Soren to motion that we should run. He stares at me with wide eyes, as though only spoken words can solve this dilemma. But I'm so out of breath myself that I can't say anything. All I can do is smell. My nostrils burn, and I think maybe something horrible and unforgivable has been dumped into the sewers. My nose activates, my olfactory pathways initiating and synthesizing with the mask's o-tech, and I pick up on the acrid, chemical scent—one I had smelled before when I was with Gherus.

Ratsbane. A type of poison for vermin.

In my confusion, I struggle to track what's happening. Strange translucent balls skitter across the concrete floor followed by violet plumes of smoke rising like angry serpents.

The effect of the smoke is immediate.

My body feels like it's attacking itself as my intestines clench and unbelievable heat roils through me. The world darkens, and an unknowable fear grips me as another dark force rips reality away. My mother's face swims into my memory, but before I can really see her or feel the warmth of her smile, the poison paralyzes me and brings me down, and she's ripped away from me too.

FOUR

The sharp taste of cinnamon stings my nasal cavity from my nose to the back of my throat, releasing me from the tight embrace of paralysis. I open my eyes and wince away hot tears. My mouth is so dry it feels like I've swallowed wool. I try opening it, desperate for water. In that first terrifying moment of waking up and realizing life is not at all what it seems, I'm desperate for many things.

There are so many answers I still want.

"Soren," I say, my voice faint. For now, I need to get us out of danger.

Light streams through an opening fifty feet above me. I can feel the darkness melting away, but the sensation is superficial. The airborne poison has burrowed into my being so deeply that I can't lift my limbs. I'm lying on a thin foam mat, the compact kind I often see at markets as a place to dry fish, or a placemat for trinkets and art. Water pushes its sludgy path beside me, but my own body awareness tells me we are in a different chamber than where we fought. I wonder what happened to the joykillers. They wouldn't have used poison. What in Crown's name is going on?

"Soren," I say, trying to lift my head.

"He took it a lot harder than you," comes a man's gravelly voice. It's familiar, but it holds a darker, sharper edge now.

I can't see the man, and I need to—I need answers more than ever now because every second without them is a second closer to losing someone else I love. Where is Soren? The man whispers something to someone else. Then I hear the scampering of footsteps, echoing through the tunneled chambers like a distant dream.

I push myself to my elbows with some effort. The world greets me with a sickening swirl and the urge to vomit grips my stomach. Taking deep breaths, I try to locate Soren and the man, who is sitting cross-legged on the ground turning over a mask in his hands. He's inspecting it like Gherus would inspect one of my inventions—carefully, like I'd embedded secrets inside of it and he needed to find them.

I touch my face and realize I'm no longer wearing my mask. Everything about this situation unsettles me, but I don't have the strength to stand. "Where's Soren?" My voice is gaining strength. I point my question at our small-faced friend like a blade.

The man's gaze lifts to meet me, but he does not move his head. He motions with the slightest nod to my left. I notice he's holding a hand tool that looks like a key, but the pointed end is wide and flat and flashes yellow and purple dots of light.

I turn and see Soren lying down on his own mat. His eyes are closed.

"What happened?" I sit up, my body trembling and on the verge of illness—the kind that keeps you weak and in bed for days. "What happened to those joykillers?"

"Joykillers?" The man asks. "Those guards who crashed our party down here? Well, you won't have to worry about them anymore." He flashes a wide-toothed grin, then lifts his head from what he's doing to look at me. "You two should be more careful. This old rat won't always be around to save you."

"It was you? With the poison?"

"I like to think of it more as an antidote." The man's smile widens.

"An antidote to what?" I reach for my mask again at my waist but find nothing.

"To the ego of man. Ratsbane is the great equalizer. No one can resist its influence."

I take several deep breaths, wondering if my own mask has helped or hindered me during the attack. Did my sensors pick up the scent and bring the fumes into my lungs more quickly? My mask's olfactotech field of apprehension is extensive, but I don't know the intricacies of this question.

As though the man can read my mind, he says, "You recovered much more quickly than I've seen. Must have something to do with this mask here."

"Give them back," I say, perhaps too forcefully, but I don't care. This guy poisoned my brother and me, and I was beginning to wish we'd never come down here.

His gaze rests on me in that same intense way, his bulbous nose bisecting his beady-eyed face. "Hey bub, you're on my turf. Same as those plated fellas. I call the shots down here, you understand?"

I don't reply. It's easy to see why Soren made his insult earlier.

"I saved your wicked lives," he says. "Maybe you should say 'thank you.'"

I bite down hard on my anger, realizing I'm in no position to argue. "Thank you. Who are you? We both hate the Crown, so it makes sense why you saved us, but—"

"Makes sense?" the man interrupts. "Makes sense? Listen here, boy. Nothing makes sense in this world. Not up there, not down here. There is no fairness, no equality, only entropy and order doing their forever dance. Our births and lives are random, and the only difference between you and me lies in chance. You need to understand this if you want to live. Today, or any other day."

Is he threatening me? I almost take the bait, but I'm interrupted again—this time by Soren.

"What the frack happened?" The poison knocked him down, but his voice still booms with power. He wipes sweat from his forehead. His innocent and empty gaze is somewhat endearing, but I'm too pissed and confused to let it reach me right now. "This guy?" Soren says, once he notes where we are. "You throw them little poison balls?"

The man stands, holding both of our masks. My body tenses up. Anger and helplessness collide as two orbiting bodies suddenly lock together.

"You both should learn some manners. Those killers of joy, as you call them, were about to wipe these sewers with you. My 'poisons' saved your life."

He holds both of the masks out in front of him as though they are expensive purchases in a luxury store, and he's trying to decide which one he wants. My body is still so weak I can't even stand up. Soren must have been worse off than me since he was out longer. We are not in a good position.

The rat man takes a slow step toward us. "I know who you boys are. Most of the capital will by now. You banged things up pretty good." He whistles sharply through his teeth. The sound is unpleasant, like our entire sewer experience. "You broke all the gauntlet rules, and both of you made out with your lives. For that, I gotta say, I'm impressed. You started a revolution, but you already know that. So far, you've gotten exactly what you want."

I disagree with the man's use of "exactly" but I'm not in a position to split hairs. In fact, the hairs on my body stand on edge and prickle with a type of uncertainty I cannot name. Everything I know is in the context of the Crown and what they can or can't do, but this man is a random entity.

I'm beginning to understand that even these chaotic events have an order to them. My brain picks out details about the rat man. There is still so much I need to learn. His accent is… northern? He must know the sciences based on the balls he threw, and I'm beginning to have a feeling—the pinpricks of light emitting from his hand tool emerge as a memory in my brain—that he knows the tech behind our masks too. At least the basics.

"But," the man goes on. "Unlucky for you, what you did doesn't just affect the Crown or Harvest and the next four years. Your stunt will affect our entire nation."

"Easy for you to pin such a heavy weight on us," Soren says. "While you hide in the shadows poisoning people."

The man glares at Soren and laughs a little too hard, tossing his head back with a jolt. "You aren't the brighter one, so lemme spell it out for you." He shows his teeth, pointed, pearly white daggers in the cave of his small mouth. "They will hunt you forever until you're ash. Burn you and everyone in your family to the ground. The revolution has begun, and it rests with you two." His tone lightens, and his scowl becomes something like a smile. At least I think it's a smile. "But you gotta get smarter if you're going to win this."

Soren and I exchange a glance. Blood and warmth return to my fingers. I wonder if it's because of this simple admission of hope by a stranger.

He tosses our masks back to us like they are supper plates. Mine lands with a thud on the mat in front of me, the lynx's features sharp and convincing in the dim light. I look at Soren and his mask, then turn to look back at the man. "You... fixed his?"

He nods. "That's right. They're quite intelligent pieces, those two."

"That how you knew we were the brothers in the gauntlet?" Soren's eyes are bright.

"No," the man says. "When I said you need to get smarter, I meant that you need to understand everything about what the Crown has given you. Your weapons. Those masks."

I feel a sinking weight in my stomach, a sack of stones plummeting to the bottom of a pond. "Oh no," I say, looking at Soren. "That's how the joykillers found us. Our masks have trackers in them."

"Had trackers in them," the man says. "I destabilized them. Now hurry up and get outta here before you attract any more goons."

I want to sprint out of there faster than any lynx can, but my arms are still cold and weak. Slowly, I bring the mask to my face. The neuralink brushes against my temples, the heavy casing merges as one with my face, and my world changes. Endorphins and testosterone flood my body. Nausea and uncertainty drain away as my aura field activates and adrenaline pushes me to stand. Soren stands across from me, his mask secured to his face as his holoskin activates and he becomes a furrier version of himself. My brother is the bear again.

"Thank you," I say, my own voice robust and ripe with power. "We won't bother you again."

The man smiles, and I like him again.

"Somehow, I doubt that," he says.

FIVE

Beyond the chamber where we've left our new friend, the passages elongate into black and hollow vortices, as though we're hurtling ourselves into space, but on foot. Lamplights blink and sputter as we walk past gnarled patches of moss spread across the walls, each with their own signature pattern.

I touch my mask, assuring myself that it's still on my face as the abyss swallows us further into its endless esophagus. My own throat and nasal cavity, battered and weak, warm as my mask continues to change my biochemistry, pumping me full of oxytocin, serotonin, and new blood cells. Soren and I grow stronger, and so does the sound of the violin music, which we locate after what seems to be an eternity of walking down and through nondescript chambers.

A white-haired woman sits with her back against the sewer walls, legs crossed underneath her, as she draws the bow across the strings of the rickety violin. She doesn't look up when we climb the landing. Soren and I stand there, brushing debris and dirt from our bodies, captured by her raw, melancholic melody.

I haven't heard music like hers in a long time. Mom drifts into my memory, and the days of hearing the piano's soft crescendo floating through our window. She would hum to herself, dancing as though she were the wind itself while she went about her chores. The twin melodies of guilt and longing play on my own heart strings then. I miss my mother terribly. I wonder how old she looks now, or if her hair is ivory white like this woman's.

The song ends and the woman looks up at us. Her eyes are like bulbous moons, wet with the sheen of self-inflicted tears. Why do humans always make themselves sad? She lays the violin across her lap, mouth agape, the surprise of two gauntlet champions standing before her settling on her face as she says, "Who are you gentlemen?" Her voice is hard, iron-wrought with pain and regret.

"How do we get out of here?" Soren asks, ignoring her question.

I look at him, half respecting his no-nonsense attitude, half regretting his tone.

The woman blinks, her eyelids heavy. "You want to get out of the city then? Is that it? I haven't seen masks like the ones you wear in a long time."

There's a long pause. The only audible sound is the trickle of water dripping from different heights into puddles and canals alike to create the smallest symphony.

"We're trying to get out of these sewers," I say. "We can't stay in the city anymore. Could you help us?"

The woman looks away. "My son fought in the gauntlet too," she says.

Soren and I exchange glances behind our masks. I wasn't expecting her to say anything like this. Of course, people are related to fighters in the gauntlet. I made a speech about that very thing earlier today, but I had never met anyone affected by the tournament before. Except for Soren. And this woman.

Some of the other champions I've defeated roll through my memories—sons and daughters of people here in the capital—and it feels like there's a clamp around my heart.

"That was a long time ago," she continues. "Those masks of yours have seen some upgrades, but through the years it's amazing how they've stayed the same. You're a bear." She squints at me. "And you must be… a puma?"

"Lynx," I say, proud of my totem and its rarity. I like that not everyone can identify what I am. The bear is a powerful totem, but it's common and predictable. I like that the lynx has never won before.

"A lynx? Ah, I see it now," the woman says. Behind her, light seems to dull and dim like the slow dying of a bulb. Outside, night is deepening. I don't want to sleep down here and know our window to leave is dwindling. "That's a rather interesting totem," she says, her eyes holding the twinkle of unspoken secrets.

"Listen, lady," Soren begins. I want to cut him off for fear of him offending our guide out of here, but he says, "We're going to bring the Crown down and avenge your son—avenge everyone's sons and daughters—but we gotta regroup. Get out of here and come back when we're ready and have a plan. We gotta get out now. Please tell us the way."

She freezes then, and I notice it happens at the mention of her son. Her gaze hardens, as though only she can talk about his memory. Then she seems to snap out of her reverie and stands, laying her violin on the ground in front of her.

"Very well. Follow the light down this tunnel," she says, pointing behind her. "There will be another crossroads when you stand under the light, but take the ladder that leads to the edge of the Southern Gate, which will be the path to your right. Take it all the way down until you reach a chamber with rushing water. You'll hear it, even now as you approach the light. That water leads to the sewer's drainage, a waterfall leading to a pool that you don't want to find yourself in—one, because of the sludge and two, because of the crocs that rule those waters. You'll see the ladder to the left of that stream. Don't you boys fall in."

Soren nods. "Thanks, Grams." He walks away toward the light.

I sigh. "Thank you for your help. We'll be back someday."

She says nothing but turns to watch as I follow Soren. When I look back, she wears a crooked smile, and I wonder if there is something she isn't telling us.

I don't have to wait too long to get that answer.

When we reach the light and look up, I can see metal grates covering the ground about twenty feet up. Dozens of feet pass above us as the din of day dwindles into the calm of night. The sun's final rays glint through the opening, casting fleeting shadows on the sewer walls around us like golden, dancing flames. Soren and I have both removed our masks. He looks at me, one eyebrow raised, like he has something to say, but then I realize he's looking past me.

"Who are you?" Soren asks.

I turn toward what he's looking at and am unsettled by what I see.

Three figures stand at the end of the chamber, staring at us. They're cloaked in shadow, each of them a height similar to my own. I can't tell their gender from where they stand, but then one of them steps forward into the half-light and my unsettled feelings morph into something more fearful—the same feeling I get when I step into the Fall Gauntlet arena. Defeat your enemy before they defeat you. The newcomer wears something on his face.

A mask—in the image and likeness of a rat.

There's more than one. Rats. The other two step forward and their outlines are more pronounced now, so still and ebony, like black bones.

"Say something!" Soren's voice is monstrous and heavy, as though its own weapon.

The one in the middle approaches us. Soren and I look at each other. I grip my gem staff as uncertainty tightens its grip on me.

The man speaks. "You boys and us rats—we have a lot in common." He continues his slow saunter toward us and at that moment, I know who is behind the mask. "We both hate the Crown and want to take them down. But do you want to know the difference between us down here and you"—he gazes up at the suggestion of light now dimming in the hollow chamber—"up there?"

"You smell like shite, and we can take baths," Soren says.

The man stops walking and jerks his head to his side as though he's been slapped, but he turns to motion to the two other rats. They all wear skin-tight clothing, black as night.

"You're that guy from before," I say, finding my voice. Exhaustion is taking me, but I won't give up here, not after everything we've done to escape. "Why are you playing with us? Let us leave."

"Now you're asking the important questions. Why indeed?" I can't see his face, but I can hear his voice sneaking out of his wide-toothed grin to greet us.

There's a pause, a moment of silence. Water drips from the walls, and I can hear it—the rushing of water beyond where they stand. Our way out. The man withdraws something from his dark, skintight suit, which eclipses into the backdrop as one image, obscuring my view. The masks seem to float, with their long, pointed rat ears, soft pink noses, whiskers, and bright, knowing eyes.

He holds a translucent ball in his hand. I can see the purple bulb inside, that once activated, will release some kind of poisonous gas to debilitate us. This is not something I've seen in the gauntlet, which is almost entirely hand-to-hand combat, except for the rare occurrence of projectile weapons like a boomerang or bow. He has already taken us down once without even a fight. I'm not about to let him do it again.

Soren and I both put our masks back on as the rat man prattles on.

"Because… you should learn some manners," the rat man says. "It just so happens that I am willing to teach you."

"I'll knock your head off!" Soren's voice rumbles through the sewers. I don't need my mask's precognition to know that Soren is about to charge the man and throw us into battle.

"Soren, wait!" My mask's o-tech activates and is already interpreting probabilities.

Razor-thin vectors burst from my visual cortex, elongating then collapsing back into the aura field as though I'm seeing a planet's rotational orbit in hyper-speed. What I see is strange. My first thought is that my mask has been tampered with. The vectors pulse then die, and the aura field before me, the second reality lying atop the first, falls like a stone from the sky as if the capital's power plant has been shut off, and I am plunged into darkness.

The world goes quiet.

In the span of a millisecond, I ingest all of this data and am surprised to see, as I turn toward Soren, vectors rising and falling around him like a maelstrom of autumn leaves. That is not the most surprising thing. The most surprising thing is that all his potential actions are directed at me.

Soren groans and grabs at his mask on both sides, trying to pull it off. I'm equally confused in that first horrifying moment, knowing that we have enemies everywhere and trust is a thing we can only share with each other. I turn to the rat man as Soren fights off whatever demon is invading his mind now.

"What did you do?" I yell at the rat man, who stands there idle, chin down, watching us. I swear I can see his beady eyes glowing behind his ugly mask.

"You were followed here because of those masks you wear," the rat man says. "You rely on them. You rely on the Crown too much. If you truly want to be free, you will learn how to separate yourselves from those who control you."

"So we just get rid of the masks?" I ask, calling over Soren's shouts and moans. "They're powerful. We need them, just like our weapons."

"Make your own then," the rat man says. "Like I have."

"Why do you care?" I'm starting to agree with Soren's assessment of this man, annoyed and angry that he continues to play games with us.

"Because if you are going to help bring down the Crown, then you must learn important lessons. If you don't, you don't stand a chance."

Soren's roars pull my attention from the rat man. He's holding his mask on both sides, groaning, and gyrating as though about to fall to his knees and vomit. He's become the bear, but it's like his two halves are splitting his entire being into separate, disconnected parts. I don't know how to help him.

"Soren! What kind of sick lesson is this?" I ask the rat man. "You want to torture us?"

"No." The rat man begins backing away. "I want you to know what it feels like to be controlled so that you never have to experience it again."

I know what he means then, and I hate him for it. Soren stops screaming in his fit of rage and pain and instead he squares up to me. He grips his club in his hand, knuckles burning blood-red, and all the vectors burst into life showing me each and every possibility coming my way. The rat man didn't tamper with my mask—it's predicting as it's supposed to—but he has tampered with Soren's. To what extent, I'm about to find out.

Whatever the rat man has done, he's found a way to control my brother, just like the Crown has for so many years.

Soren charges at me, and it's like we're back in the Fall Gauntlet again, battling against each other, and caught in someone else's cruel game.

SIX

I s there something in Soren's mask that makes him easier to control, or do some people just understand his personality and use his rage against him? My aura field explodes into a mosaic of cosmic blue and white light. Vector lines materialize and give shape to the chaos, like musical notes on a scale suddenly played into existence.

Incapacitating Soren for a third time today was not part of the plan but then again neither was escaping the Fall Gauntlet with my long-lost brother and starting a revolution. Life sucks and then you die, like Dad always used to say.

I grip my gem staff, intuit correctly as to Soren's next move, throw all my weight left and dive out of his way as he barrels toward where I was standing. He's more bull than bear today, at the mercy of his own madness. I roll to my feet as Soren pivots. He releases a frustrated moan, then smacks his own head with his massive gauntlets like he's trying to knock himself out of his vile possession.

I need a way to knock Soren out while exacting the least amount of pain on him.

My aura field reaches beyond Soren to show me more probabilities, and I see the rat man fidgeting with some kind of control in his hands. An impossibly thin line threads him to Soren, and if I destroy that control, I can free my brother.

Soren stands between me and the rat man as though protecting him.

"Soren, take the mask off," I say, my breaths thick and heavy like the air around me. "He's done something to it."

"You've done something to it," Soren says, unmoving. "Why don't you take your mask off?"

I'm stunned, unsure if this is the work of the rat man's alterations or if this is Soren's true mind now given space to speak. My heart thumps in my chest. I try to slow it and calm my nerves, but I'm scared and angry and confused. My own emotions are boiling like a soup inside me, ready to overflow and burn everything in their path. "I need my mask. To see the truth."

Soren scoffs, not himself in that moment. This changed version of him has too much disgust and venom for the situation. "It's always about what you want. Never what I want," he says.

"What do you want?" The rat man's voice is thin and wispy, but it carries.

"I want to save my girlfriend," Soren says. He squares up to me, stiller and more serene than I've ever seen him, as though this admission of truth is his path to freedom.

"We can't stay in the capital," I say. "I told you we'd come back for her."

"You're a liar, Benji."

His words hit me harder than any spiked club could. For a moment they paralyze me. Fear begins its work of crawling into all the crevices of my brain, injecting them with the insecurities I've worked all my life to undo.

"You told me you would come for me," Soren says. "You never did."

"Soren—" My voice catches in my throat. What's the rat man done to Soren's mask? Does it even matter anymore? There's truth in what my brother says. I feel it in the marrow of my bones, like lightning that keeps touching down in the same place, causing a rawer pain each time. I need to say something or else I will break.

"I can't," I say finally, the tightness in my throat growing even tighter. My facial muscles constrict beneath my mask. "I was a prisoner too."

Soren exhales through his nose and stares me down. The three rats remain still behind him, and the rat man is no longer fidgeting with his controls. He's angered Soren, but the real emotion in this conversation has come from a dark and painful place inside my brother.

"And yet you spent all your time trying to bring back a mother who left us. Instead of your own brother." Soren's voice drops an octave and weakens. Something inside him is cracking, and I'm about to have to pick up the broken pieces. "At least Dad was always there for us. He would have fought for us till his last breath."

"He wasn't there for Mom," I say, almost in disbelief. I've forgotten how young Soren was when Mom was taken away. I know his memories of the event aren't as strong. "He just let them take her away. And he couldn't protect us either. I didn't know what had happened to you. I didn't know that I could fight for you."

"It was all because of Mom," Soren says. "She started everything and left us first. No one was there for me."

This was really at the heart of Soren's pain: a mother, a father, and brother who had all left him. Was the rat really able to trigger all of this just by altering his mask? If so, there are many things about o-tech that I still don't understand.

I can't lose my brother over it though.

Soren tightens his gauntlets into fists and raises his chin at me. "No one except for Abbi. And you want to leave her behind too."

Before I can answer, Soren charges. A millisecond before he moves, my aura field expands into the probability universe I'm so used to seeing. The vector lines rise like waves then crash, but I know Soren's style—he's direct and will go straight for my throat.

Which is what he's doing now.

He closes the distance between us and is upon me, swiping his huge claws again. I sidestep, then launch myself backward from his next attack and ready my gem staff. I slide the top part of the shaft down my hands to give myself more range, grip the end with both hands like I'm swinging a bat, building up kinetic energy, then swing at his arms as he comes at me again. My staff slams into his bicep hard enough to shatter fortified glass, and he groans. I swing it hard and know he'll bruise from it, but I can't be slowed down by emotion. I have to end his tirade so I can go after the rat man and finally get some answers.

A guttural sound emerges from Soren's throat. "Abbi's the one who's always been there for me. She's the one I want to save!"

I can't allow this stunt to steal my brother away. "We'll save her, Soren. I promise that we will. We just need to escape the city right now."

Soren's swiping at me again. He charges and barrels into my frame throwing me back. I stay light on my feet, but nearly trip over from the force. He advances again, his rage hot and revived, his huge body looming over me in the dying light.

"Your mask has been tampered with," I say. "By them." I point at the rat men behind Soren. "This isn't you. Please listen to me."

Soren's claw whirls past my face in a rush of energy. He nicks skin on his second swipe, cutting my neck and drawing first blood. One inch closer and he'd have sliced my throat and drowned me in my own blood.

"No more talking," Soren says. "I'm sick of all the words you use, brother."

I have to know what the rat has done, and I need to find out fast. My aura field expands and collapses like lungs pumping oxygen through the body of the sewers. Ingesting the probabilities, I know debilitating Soren is the only way. We parry and jostle in an anxious fit of jabs and swings. My body sings an exhausted song, and the words grow fainter. It's already been one hell of a day, and all I want is to get out of the dingy sewers alive with my brother.

Soren invades my space again, his claws now reaching out like hands, jabbing and punching. When his rage dissipates for the tiniest moment—the vector lines lying flat in my immediate aura field—I take the opening.

Stepping back and away, I feint right with my staff, then whip my body around to the left side, drawing an arc with my staff behind me and smack the gem into Soren's left thigh. His roar of pain crushes my heart. I don't want to injure my brother any more than I already have, but I have no choice.

When he goes down, I become a torpedo of energy, shooting through the sewers like a beam of light at the rat man and his sidekicks.

"Stop!" The rat man's screech punctuates the near silence.

I do not stop.

"Stop right there, or I blow up your brother's mask while it's still on his face," the rat man says.

That gets my attention.

The vector lines in my aura field activate, lapping like waves against the shore, slow but constant. I still don't know what the rat man has done to Soren's mask, but I can't risk walking away without knowing. I stop before I know what's happening. The rat man holds that same key device in his hand and lifts it, as though ready to press a button any second. Has he added some kind of explosive to it?

"What do you want?" I ask. My voice is steady, but behind the guise of control lies my own dormant rage. I'm tired of being controlled by other people. "What threat do we pose to you, anyway? Stop your games and let my brother go!"

Soren moans behind me. I can hear the clench of his teeth biting back pain.

The rat man steps forward. His two accomplices remain at rest behind him, their eyes twinkling like stars in the sewer's dark abyss. "I'll free your brother and allow you to pass safely through the sewers under one condition."

"Say it!"

"Give up your masks."

Soren's labored breathing dots this new silence, this new fateful direction that we do not seem to have a choice in.

"You always have a choice," Gherus had said. "When it comes to loved ones and family, you can always choose the right thing—but that thing may not always keep you alive."

I can see Master Gherus standing in his cluttered shop, and I can still feel his care for me, even after all this time.

"Never," I say. "These masks are our only chance at overthrowing the Crown. I'd never give them away to you."

"Suit yourself," the rat man says. The vector lines surge and billow out from the concentric focal point, and I intuit that whatever he's about to do will have dire consequences. He holds his hand up high, like he's going to press some instant-death button, eyes gleaming.

"Wait!" I hold out my hand for him to hold off. "Why?" My breathing is erratic, and I'm sputtering. "Why do you want our masks?"

"My motives are my own," the rat man says, his voice venomous. "Maybe I don't want to have to worry about you screwing up my plans. Maybe I want you to learn that the Crown will always control you as long as you're attached to people you care about. Maybe I'm still making my mind up about you."

I turn to Soren, whose pain seems to be deepening. He's on his hands and knees, seething, suffering. I don't know where his physical pain ends and where his emotional and psychological pain begin. Truth is, Soren probably doesn't know either.

"Soren, are you still in there?" I ask.

"What'll it be?" the rat man asks. "Time to make a decision."

I'm frozen, paralyzed by fear, much like Dad was the day they took Mom away. Part of me knows what that felt like now. Maybe Dad said nothing in that moment because he knew he had to lose Mom in order to save us. I don't know what we can do without our masks. The idea of taking down the Crown as just Soren and Benji scares me. My heartbeat quickens as I stand at this fateful crossing, as the vector lines lower and float to baseline.

A calm before the storm.

I've fought so long and so hard to get my brother back, but is it I who did it, or was it the lynx?

The rat man laughs with scorn. "You say you want your family back and yet you can't even trade your mask for your brother. What will you do, Benji, when the time comes for you to free your mother?"

"How do you know about my mother?"

"You're a Fall Gauntlet champion—well, nearly. Wake up, Benji. Anyone smart enough to plan a rebellion ought to know all the important pieces during this next Harvest, and you surely are one of them. It doesn't take much to learn a person's history if you know the right people to ask. Don't you know that rats are everywhere?"

I don't know what to say. My head throbs with information overload, and my heart knots like the crooked roots of a tree in my chest—frustration that I'm again at the mercy of someone else boils inside me.

"What'll it be?" I know it's the last time the rat man will ask this question.

I have no more fight left for this unsavory stranger. I remove my mask and chuck it across the sewer floors like it's a timebomb waiting to self-destruct. The rat man grins in the eerie darkness and presses a button on his device. Soren inhales air sharply behind me as though he's just been held underwater for minutes and can finally breathe again. He gasps and has a coughing fit. The rats recover his mask too, and then they all walk off, but not before the rat man says, "Glad you came to your senses. Now you're finally free."

Somehow, it doesn't feel like the freedom I've imagined.

SEVEN

I tend to Soren after the final footsteps of our rat adversaries echo into nothing, but my brother is in bad shape. He's lying face-up on the cold, damp stone with his arms above his head, breaths shallow, eyes wide open. When I kneel beside him, he barely acknowledges me.

"Soren, are you okay?" I ask. "What'd he do to your mask?"

After a moment, he side-eyes me and registers that he's not alone. His breath slows, and he begins exhaling through his nose. He's clenching his jaw, holding back something that I cannot place. I'm beginning to see that I don't know the shape, size, and color of Soren's pain. I haven't really touched it, don't yet know the texture or the weight of what he carries with him, but I understand that his greatest pains would not be physical. All his pain lives in the form of ghosts that he thinks he's vanquished. I understand that I am one of those ghosts.

"You left me," Soren says, and he breaks then.

He grabs his face with monstrous hands and cries into them. His mouth open, he runs his hands up his sideburns to grab his hair and cries in an attempt to release some of the pain he's been holding onto for more than half his life. When I see my brother in that horrible, confused state, I want to cry too. I almost do, but I hold back my pain because Soren becomes my world then. All that matters is understanding and comforting him.

"I'm sorry, Soren," is all that I can say. Glimpses of us in our old apartment flash through my brain as pieced-together memories, like my aura field with the quick, tepid vector lines falling then lurching through the tundra of my mind. An aura field I will likely never see again. My own throat tightens, and I battle for breath. "I'm so sorry," I say, trying to assure him that I am but failing miserably. Soren cries, his face blanched white. I grab his hands, cold and meaty, in mine. I touch his forehead and feel how hot it is.

"You're feverish," I say, still afraid of what the rat man has done to him—what sort of dark memories he has unleashed into the world that is Soren. "Soren, listen. I'm so sorry. I was only ten. I was traumatized. I lost all of you too. I didn't know what was happening, how to mourn you, how to find you, so I did the only thing I knew to do and that was start at the beginning. Start where the Crown had started. They'd taken Mom first. She'd been gone longer."

The love I felt for Mom was more primal and deeply rooted than the love I felt for Soren. The fact that Soren and I could work together to rescue Mom had never occurred to me, but I can't tell Soren that—not in his current state.

"I figured the more time that went on without her, the greater the chances of losing her. She was the one who needed saving. We were slaves to the Crown. I can't explain what was happening, but please know I'd never abandon you. Never. I'm here now, and I won't lose you again." I hold back the flood of my own pain, but water is breaking through the dam. Guilt, shame, and regret stretch me into an unrecognizable shape. "Okay?"

My own tears start just as Soren's seem to be drying up. I fall onto his chest and cry and the darkness I feel and see is absolute. I black out, lose track of time, and don't know if I'm still in the sewers or running through my own dark and wicked past that seems endless.

I come to, waking up to Soren's hands holding mine. His breathing steadies as we sit up and hold each other, as the elusive and mysterious goddess of time continues to charge ahead without us. Soren's skin is icy, then hot enough to burn metal. He vomits and his body goes slack against my now fragile frame.

"We have to get you out of here," I say, trying to stand.

Soren nods and slowly rises to his feet. I want the rat man to pay for what he's done, but I know getting Soren well and to safety is our priority.

As is our luck, it doesn't happen quite like that.

We make it to the part of the sewer where the tunnel opens to the outside. Water rushes out into a dimly lit sky, down into a river where crocs live and devour their prey. The sun is coming up, pouring its brilliant white-yellow rays onto a world that will never truly live under its light.

When I look out past the sewer's final opening into the river and barren lands leading into savannah, I feel the slightest tinge of hope—hope that piece by piece, if we do all the right things at the right times, we can bring down the Crown.

Soren's cough brings me back to the present. I see the ladder to the left of the sewer's opening to the outside world, chained to the only part of the sewer wall that hasn't been blasted away. It's strange seeing such lush nature ahead of us while still being technically underground. The ladder's twenty metal rungs are thin and brittle like tree branches, and I'm not sure they can even hold Soren. There's still the issue of getting him to the ladder. He's on his knees again, his hands clutching the cold, wet ground in silent pain.

"Soren, we're almost out of here. Let's get you up that ladder. Okay?"

"You might have more success launching yourselves into the river. You'll die either way, but the river will be quicker than what I'm about to do to you."

I don't know how it happens or when the rat man arrives, but his voice presses into my skull like ten thousand nails, and I feel like my rage will destroy any semblance of sanity I still hold onto. My brain wants to explode. I don't want to have to think anymore. Exhaustion grips my body, and my thoughts spiral.

"Kill him, Benji," Soren says. He's trying to prop himself up on his elbows. His head is shaking, no—trembling, as if he will vomit any second.

My rage becomes adrenaline and everything inside me alights like a phoenix rising from the burning embers of this past twenty-four-hour hellfire. The rat man is nowhere that I can see. I swing my gaze around me. All that matters is finding him. He's not on the ladder nor is he standing at the edge of the sewer's naked opening. I walk over and look down, my skin crawling with bloodthirst. To my left, the rush of water from the canal tumbles over the edge and empties into the river fifty feet down as mist and spray roil back up toward us.

"What did you do to my brother?" My rage is a monster slowly showing its face. Still, I cannot see the rat man, but I feel his presence stronger than ever.

"You know, when I heard about the lynx, I was expecting someone much smarter." The rat man emerges from a pocket of shadow in his sleek, black uniform and of course, his rat mask. This is an enemy I am done underestimating, so I quickly note everything I can about him. Soren's life depends on it.

In the several hours since I've last seen the rat man, he's beefed up. He's still short, but I can make out muscle definition in his quads and biceps. I track his small movements, as if I am still wearing my mask, trying to intuit any action he might take, probabilities and outcomes racing through my mind. He wants to talk, so I let him, while I analyze him and try to identify potential weak points.

"Then I met you, and you didn't even know how to get out of the sewers without help. You didn't know that the Crown was tracking you with these." He holds up both my mask and Soren's. They hang lifeless from the cradle of his fingertips. "In fact, you didn't even really know the most basic elements of how your masks work or did what they did."

That isn't entirely true, but I let him continue. For him to have grown like he has in such a short time, I know he's taken some kind of enhancements, but I don't know which ones. It occurs to me then that maybe he's right, and there are still many things I don't know about. From now on, I won't remain naïve about what else is out there.

"We don't need those," I say. "Tell me what you did to my brother, and you can leave with your pathetic life."

The rat man steps closer. Soren lifts his head to look at him and spits.

"You might want to rethink whose life is pathetic in this case," the rat man says. "Allow me to introduce myself, Benji." I feel as though this is some sick joke, another plan orchestrated by the Crown to hurt my family, and my stomach lurches as I smell the poison gas again, my olfactory senses activating from the recent memory.

Soren and I both stare at this toxic stranger and wait.

"My name is Dr. Tanner Fitz. Most of my life I was dedicated to the sciences. Ten years ago, the Crown identified me as talent, and I was brought under their great establishment, commandeered to perform experiments. I won't get into all the gritty details here, but needless to say, I was asked to do things I had never done before. In time, these experiments wore on my soul. Yes, I was born with a soul, and even now, I struggle to keep mine alive." The rat man—Dr. Fitz—lowers his chin and glares at me from behind his stupid mask. "At one point, I was a very powerful man within the Crown's service. They discovered this. They learned that I had uncovered new technologies that would bring their nation much-needed change."

I hate listening to this man talk, but I know what he has to say is important. A day ago, I needed to know how to attain more influence and power. I thought it only existed in the Crown or the gauntlet champions, but here was another avenue: scientists.

I find myself listening and staring as the sun comes up behind me, warming me into a state of half-submission.

"And now you live in the sewers as a thorn in the Crown's side," I say, unable to stop myself. I need answers faster. "You couldn't do what they asked you to do anymore, so you changed sides. So, why hasn't the Crown ended you?"

"They thought they did." The rat man steps closer. Both of our masks hang in his hands like lifeless ornaments. "They observed my dead body and could not refute what they saw. With the help of my rat allies, my body was rescued and the Crown went on with their business, with no knowledge of what had happened."

I imagine this man lying dead in the streets, chemicals stalling his heart to nothing, appearing dead but truly alive.

"I was safe and thriving down here," the rat man says, his voice holding off a surge of anger. "Until you came along and tipped off the Crown to my whereabouts." He dips his chin again and widens his stance. "You will pay for your transgressions." He throws both masks. They slide across the sewer floor, stopping mere feet from me. "You will fight me," he says. "Only one of us can live and become the Fall Gauntlet champion."

"Fall Gauntlet champion?" I ask, dumbfounded. "The Fall Gauntlet is over. These sewers have nothing to do with the tournament."

"Didn't I tell you that the Crown will get their champion, one way or another?"

I pick up our masks, knowing that death will close in on Soren if I don't get a grip on my present reality. Avoiding the Fall Gauntlet was something I could never do. Why would now be any different? Dr. Fitz stares at me, and it occurs to me that something has changed in the last two hours. "They found you—the Crown. They told you to take me down."

"No," Dr. Fitz says. "I will no longer be the Crown's instrument. I chose the rat totem myself. I was training for the next Fall Gauntlet, you idiot, and now you've wrecked everything. I will not relinquish my rat identity or what I've worked so hard to build."

"You were training for the next Fall Gauntlet?" Now I can see that he's using his mask for that purpose.

"I didn't think I'd qualify because I didn't have one of the Crown's masks," Dr. Fitz says. "They're special. They have special technologies, ones I have been trying to replicate for years. And then you two came along with gauntlet masks, the missing piece to a puzzle I've been trying to solve my entire life. How can someone physically small and weak oppose someone much stronger, bigger, and faster?" Dr. Fitz's body continues to grow, muscle by muscle, as though he's being injected with hormones.

I try to recall the rat in *The Book of Totems* and what it signifies, but Dr. Fitz tells me. He's no longer the rat man, but the rat itself, squaring up to me as my next opponent. I notice tiny vials of milky blue liquid strapped to his forearm and know he's getting the contents into his body somehow, either through drinking them or through a needle.

"The rat shall bring evolution of a different kind, but it shall be by my hand, and not the Crown's," he says.

"Then you're no different than them," I say. "You're a coward, using painful memories or devices to control people." I toss Soren's mask to him, but it lands with a thud beside him as he clutches at the ground with white knuckles. "You say you want to take the Crown down, but at first chance, you rejoin them."

"You don't understand because you're still a child," the rat says. "I don't have a choice because you were too stupid to know that you were being tracked. Now they know I'm alive. I had everything planned out. Now, those plans have been accelerated. I can either end you now or be destroyed by the Crown. What would you do if you were me?"

We've talked enough. I know the Crown's antics well enough to know that Dr. Fitz is right. My only regret is trusting him and taking too long to exit the sewers.

The sun is hot on my back. Soren is deathly ill, scraping by as life escapes his body. I see him grab the mask, stare at it, bring it to his face. As I watch him struggle with what to do, I realize that I have not really escaped the Fall Gauntlet. Only the arena has changed.

Does the Crown want Soren and me to face off until one of us is dead? Are adversaries like the rat meant to push us to battle each other once more?

The rat is upon me before I have any answers to my questions.

I push out the toxic chemicals that invade my nostrils with a strong exhale, pressing my own mask to my face, and keep exhaling until integration is complete. The world explodes into a kaleidoscope of probabilities as the aura field around me grows into its own cosmic, white-blue universe. I'm not sure if my mask has been tampered with, but I don't have a choice at this point. I need to see the rat's potential moves in order to take him down, and I need to do it quickly.

My olfactory senses are taking a beating as scent after scent roil past me and through me. Some of the scents are delayed or blocked by my mask's ventilation system. Whatever acidic smell is now invading my skull can—no, will—take me down in minutes if I don't cut off its source.

I intuit Dr. Fitz sliding between my legs, snatch at his collar and hold him up as though he's a ragdoll. He's light and thin, child-like even. I hold his small body with ease, as Soren once held mine, and push out the smells with strong bursts of air from my nostrils. He must have become immune to whatever smells he is putting out in the years he's spent building his own mask. What has he learned from stealing our masks? Is his weapon an array of toxic poisons?

He kicks at me with quick thrusts of his feet and claws at my hand as I hold him in place. Swinging his momentum up, he wraps his legs around my torso and bites my wrist.

The pain—his small, kernel-like teeth sinking through my gauntlets into my skin—is instant but minor. I grip his throat and throw him into the sewers to my right, knowing that if either of us find ourselves in the rushing filth of sewer water, we'll be swept down and away into the great river below.

New pains begin to set in as I wait for him to surface or be swept away. I wait. My wrist stings as though there is still a creature attached to my flesh, digging deeper every second. The vector lines in my aura field morph from sky blue to forest green. I lack the understanding to know what is happening with my mask's o-tech, but I know my body. With a sudden horror, my stomach reels. I clutch it, haunted by the realization that I have been poisoned.

I panic.

I fish Dr. Fitz out of the sewers. He's in my hands one moment, then through them, slipping out of reach like a buttery fish. And yet, this fish has the tail of a rat—things seem to be growing and evolving on him as I watch.

"Does your poison have the power to change what I see?" I ask him, unable to stop myself.

He scoffs at me and says, "People have always crushed rats under their heel, forever using them to their wicked ends." He stands at the other end of the tunnel, his body shape morphing in long shadows cast against the far wall like giant, inverted teardrops. Water drips from his elongating body. "And through it all, rats survive and evolve. They're perfect. Unlike humans, they perform the task at hand without excess or waste. I find it fitting that a rat should decide what kinds of memories and hormones humans should get, and when!"

"What did you do to me?" My aura field shows the high probability of me staggering, then falling, but I fight it, and stand my ground. Fever rolls through my weakening body.

"What I should have done as soon as I met you," the rat says. "When it comes to one's own life, we can't take chances. Wouldn't you agree, Benji?"

I follow his voice, but my sight is starting to waver. The aura field is still visible but the layer of reality beneath that—time and space and matter—is beginning to darken and thin out like a door closing out the light.

"Soren?" I call, feeling a warm blanket of darkness begin to overtake me. "Soren, I need you." Turning, I see my brother still clutching the ground, trying to rise, fingers curled around a mask that seems, for the first time ever, too heavy to lift to his face.

"You'll both die here," the rat says.

I think of Soren living so he can be with Abbi again. I think of saving Mom and Dad, of all of us together again. My entire being comes alive, and I am like fire itself.

My aura field must respond to my new burst of adrenaline because instead of bursting with possibilities and showing me more of the world in front of me, it shows me less.

Vector lines fall and others disintegrate into blackened nothingness. All that remains are a handful of equations related to my own energy inputs and corresponding outcomes.

The main probabilities.

Something in my brain has rewired—perhaps from the poison—and my entire body tightens like a gripclaw gear snapping into place.

I see what I need to do.

I dash through the sewers like a predator for its prey, swinging my gem staff around and above me, ducking down to sweep around myself in concentric circles all to create kinetic energy. I've never seen this combination of probabilities and don't always link actions together like this, but the aura field shows me this potential answer, and I follow it. My arms surge with power as I swing my staff around. The rat yells at me. He must feel the psychic energy building in the marrow of his bones. He's a man of science but could not predict this outcome.

The aura field shows him slinking, then darting, through the shadows in a beeline for Soren. He's fast—faster than me in my current state. But I don't need speed, because I have something new: electron particle electricity, something I didn't know how to use and manipulate before today.

My staff generates electricity from its gemstone and shoots through the darkened sewers at the rat man, striking him in the chest and blasting him into the wall. The sewer lights up with proto-electric static. His body jolts in response as the energy dissipates in a spider-web pattern from his chest where I've made contact. My first reaction is shock, since my staff has never generated electricity before. I don't have time to think about it. I'm on him the next moment, holding him up by the throat.

Electrical currents zip through his waterlogged body like critters fleeing a death-space. Instead of feeling the electricity still coursing through his body, faint traces run through me as they channel back to my staff, and I wonder if my mask or pure adrenaline has somehow blocked this effect. His eyes roll in their sockets until they focus on me. I know his own weapon and powers are activating, his body enlarging, ridding himself of this new, acute dose of electric shock. He glares down at me with hate in his eyes. My hands tighten but his neck responds to the grip, his own muscles bulging with the dormant water he's holding in his body.

"You poisoned me?" My fury is building. "Cure it, and I'll spare you."

He spits at me and swings his legs again, kicking. "Die! You're no champion!"

I slam his back against the wall and knock the wind out of him. His rat companions are pooling in the darkness around us. Their eyes wink into existence like dozens of lamplights suddenly lit.

"Tell me! You can still walk away with your life," I say.

Dr. Fitz's eyes are bulging within his mask, the veins in his hands saturated and huge as his body holds more and more water. If I had more time, I'd study him and his mask. Other people were making and wearing masks outside of the tournament, and something told me this wouldn't be the last enemy I'd face. The sewage water rushes behind me. I could simply dunk him into the water and hold him until he drowns, until his lungs fill with water and burst.

The river and the crocs below would take his life in an equally painful way. But he holds final answers that I need. Maybe they're embedded in his mask. Maybe I can tease them out in time, but Soren and I are on death's door. We don't have time.

I tighten my hand around his throat and fight against the water inside his body as it pushes against my own growing power. I press into his Adam's apple with my thumb. He groans and writhes like a child ready to tantrum.

"Okay," he hisses. I loosen my grip on him.

"Okay!" he says again, this time with more gusto. "Puuut me downnn," come the garbled words.

I lower the rat's dangling feet to the ground but keep my hand around his throat. We slog closer to the edge of the sewers. The sun is nearly visible, rising over an expanse of russet-green forest to the east. "Tell me now, or get ready to swim."

The rat chokes as he tries to get words out. "There is no—" He coughs again and wraps his hands around my gauntlets, as if he has some say in what happens to him. "There's no antidote or cure. I used Henephus on you. The effect is temporary. It's a poisonous mushroom but the amount in my bite wasn't enough to kill, only jam up your nervous system."

"How do I know you're not lying?" I tighten my grip around his throat with new vigor. I can see the veins around his eyes inside his mask bulge and turn purple.

"Please, don't end me like this," he croaks. "You're better than this."

As I hold this small man in my hands, ready to end his life, I wonder if he's right. In the gauntlet, I had no choice but to win to save Mom, but out here is different.

If I truly am the champion meant to win, what kind of champion do I want to be? This man has dealt with the capital too, and he escaped. There are other ways than violence and murder to deal with problems, despite what the Crown wants to teach us.

"How are we supposed to beat the Crown?" I ask. The sewage water rushes over the edge to the river below, so loud that I can hear almost nothing else. I project my voice to carry over it. "You know the Crown and their devices better than anyone." I'm beginning to understand how vital Dr. Fitz can be to our cause. "How do we bring them down?"

The rat squirms and tries to speak. "You have to leave the sewer. If I don't finish you, they'll come for all of us. They're watching this match even now."

I feel a strange tingling in my brain that's almost euphoric. I know better though. There are still so many things about my mask that I don't know. The Crown knows more than I do about the o-tech. There may be microchips and ciantech affecting my biochemistry that I know nothing about. Dr. Fitz is teaching me that.

I study the rat mask and admire its intricate design: the sharp lines and curvature of its mouth angling down, the large nose and tendril-like whiskers. With my free hand, I reach down and grab the mask from Dr. Fitz's face. I step back, releasing my hold on his neck, but with his mask in my hands.

He collapses to the ground and releases a great sigh. He coughs terribly.

"So that's it—just leave?" I ask.

"The Crown will continue to manufacture their own champions to take you down, Benji," Dr. Fitz says. He looks small and shriveled, a dried-out prune shrunken by water and days without sunlight.

"So we end their mask supply?" I wonder about the relationship between the humans that advance past the grunt rounds and the mask's tech, but there isn't time to ask.

"They get their microchips from the Tangerine Islands," he says. "There's a doctor there working for them that's skilled with nanotech. That's their source of power. Shut him down and you might start to find yourself on an even playing field."

I say nothing, still processing these new pieces of information. Soren is on his feet. His body is shaking, his mask still on the ground.

"Surely, you don't need my mask where you're going," Dr. Fitz says.

I look down at the mask in my hands. "You won't be needing it anymore. You no longer have to worry about being the Crown's chosen champion." I turn to go.

"Then you'll never find out what I did to your brother," he says.

The vector lines in my aura field surge, and in my periphery I see those probabilities gain power and steam. Dr. Fitz wants us to go, but he wants his mask more. He lunges at me as I turn back to face him. Time seems to pass in slow motion as my mask interprets every micromovement, and probability turns into fact. I have my answer as to how Dr. Fitz was getting the milky-blue liquid into his body—through a needle—which brightens like a match being struck as he swings his final weapon up in an arc.

I hate that sometimes I have no say in the order of things, and that everything I hold dear can be gone in an instant.

Soren is up and well enough to charge then. Dr. Fitz drives for my neck, his needle gleaming, but Soren is quicker. The stagnant air buzzes with the rush of his body as he barrels into Dr. Fitz and sends him over the edge. His tormented scream fills the air.

There's a loud splash, followed by the sounds of fiendish paddling and a vital life being eaten away piece by piece by crocodiles. Dr. Fitz's bloodcurdling screams are all we can hear as he struggles and fails to stay alive. I don't need to look over the sewer's edge to watch.

Soren falls into me, and I hold him up. The hundred eyes studding the darkness swirl around us like we are a black hole sucking them into orbit. The rats will make us pay for what we've done to their master.

"Soren, your mask!" I say, eyeing the ladder to our left.

Soren blinks slowly, his amber eyes riddled with pain and uncertainty. He shakes his head. He wants to leave his mask, to not be burdened by it anymore, or by anything to do with the Crown. The rats charge at us, and we parry and easily hold them off, their attacks nothing compared to the way Dr. Fitz fought. Their masks are not the real thing— they don't provide their users with supernatural abilities. They're only for show, for the appearance of unity. As soon as Soren and I break through their barrage of attacks, Soren leading and hacking away with his club, we are up the ladder as fast as our poisoned bodies can take us.

EIGHT

In the warm, brilliant sunlight of the savannah, Soren and I take turns vomiting everything inside of us onto the barren land. Below, the canyon opens up into the river, which slithers and widens as my eyes track its course through the new dry and immense land, an endless expanse of russet splotched with jade, emerald, and olive-colored plants that have evolved to survive drought and harsh winds. On the river, dark edges appear on the water's surface like serrated knives.

My stomach reels in pain each time I throw up whatever is left inside me. The hairs on my arms tingle, and my forehead is hot enough to boil tea. My entire body is burning off toxins.

Once our vomiting and coughing fits are over, Soren and I sit on the ground with our backs leaned up against one another. Everything hurts.

"We have to find you a doctor," I say. "He admitted that he did something to your mask."

Soren's breaths are shallow against the hollow of my back. We are not breathing as one. "I'm not doing so well, I think," he says.

His confession scares me.

"What about you?" Soren asks, his voice weak. "He poisoned you too."

"It's temporary. I'm starting to feel better." I remove my mask and wipe the sweat from my brow. "I don't know what town is next, but we have to keep moving. I can't leave you here." The horrifying thought that I could still lose my brother out here, away from help, away from the false security of the Crown and the capital, grips me with a cold, merciless hand.

To my surprise, Soren stands. He takes great care as he pushes himself to his feet, like a great ape waking up for the day. "Then let's keep moving," he says.

I stand but don't fully trust my legs to keep me upright. "What are you going to do without your mask?"

Soren's expression doesn't change. Our eyes meet for a moment before he reveals his mask and presses it to his face.

"Soren—!" I'm still afraid that the added effects might cripple him.

The integration process is quick but not without pain— pain that Soren seems to be holding in places he won't show me. In time, I hope he will. He starts sniffing the ground, and I see the likeness of a bear, as thick, dense hair sprouts on his mask and his holoskin activates.

"If we need to move, then let's move," Soren says. His voice is stronger in this state. I hope he isn't using it to ignore the pain and push through, but then again, we aren't left with much choice. He brought his mask with him, and even though the Crown still has a hold on me and my brother, the masks are the most powerful weapons we have. We have to use them. For now.

Soren bounds off into the vast and empty outlands as the river snakes below us. I put on my mask and follow. My eyes adjust to the day's brightness as small clouds roll overhead. The vector lines do nothing but surge forward in straight lines, reflecting the probabilities that our most advantageous motions are ahead.

I don't know how long we have, but I can hear a train horn in the distance where clouds of engine smoke billow up like puffs of poisonous gas. I know that Soren must see it too because he runs faster.

Catching the train will give us a chance to rest, and we'll get to whatever town it is going to much faster than if we are on foot.

Soren and I run as hard as we can, like we are kids again, running through the capital streets like our lives—and the lives of our parents—depend on it.

I thought taking down the rat would be the last of our Fall Gauntlet encounters, but I was about to find out just how wrong I could be.

END OF BOOK TWO

THE FALL GAUNTLET:

CHRYSIX

BOOK THREE

J. A. MERKEL

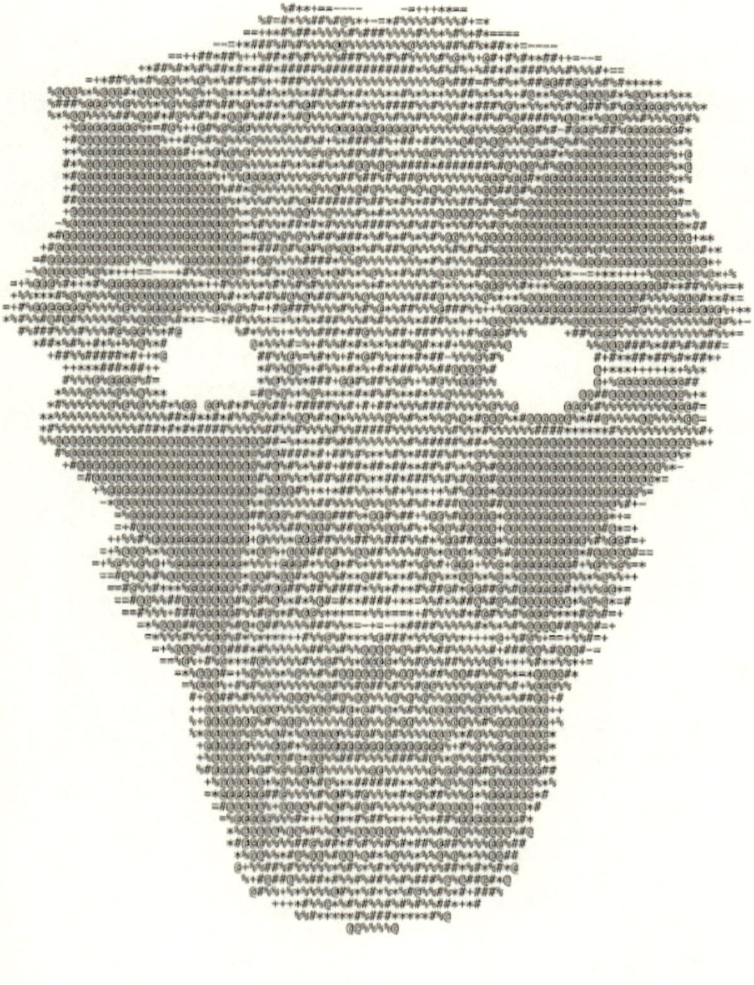

For you, reader.
No matter what you believe in, you were born with truth
inside of you. You already know the way.

CHRYSIX

It is said that the chrysix emerged as one of Calypso's rare and elusive creatures even before the beast wars began and caught like wildfire.

Would it be impossible to believe that the gods and goddesses looked down upon some creatures and blessed them with an ounce of their power?

Totem scholars believe that the chrysix was one of the Dei's most prized, that it was touched by fire and given powers of destruction and thus creation so that it could pair with a human champion and carry out their will, even after they were gone.

When the chrysix's fire keeps you warm during the cold desert night, hear its song of triumph, how it carries the torch of the divine in its belly. Feel the lash of its tongue, the sweep of its tail. Learn how it walks through fire and doesn't get burned.

That is when the chrysix rises up.
That is when the chrysix becomes you.

The Book of Totems, Chrysix

ONE

I have only seen the savannah in holopics and drawings, so when Soren and I run across it for the first time, all I think about—all I feel—is how amazing it is to be here. The air dances with the scent of dry grass, carrying melodies of chirping insects. A lone eagle's call pierces the cloudless blue sky. Here, things feel alive. I feel alive.

We escaped the capital and the Crown.

Freedom tastes like clean air and unfiltered sunlight. Also, a bit like smoke. It's so hot out here, and getting hotter, that I'm worried we aren't going to catch the train in time. The ground beneath my boots is coarse and warm, the air thick with the abrupt possibility of death.

My lynx mask brings my surroundings into sharp focus; my aura field reawakens and my senses open to what lies beyond the world I've always known. I see probabilities in the form of numbers, equations, and vector lines dancing across a blue-black horizon. When I try to parse out meaning, a recent memory hurtles into me at full speed.

Then you'll never find out what I did to your brother! the rat man had said.

Those haunting words echo across the tundra of my mind. I need to know what the rat man did to Soren and his mask. If I lose my brother because of some poison or drug, I won't be able to live with myself.

"Soren!" I call ahead, but he's a furry brown blur ahead of me. The sight of him on his feet again, active and healthy, quells the pit of uneasiness in my stomach, but I still need answers.

It seems like Soren is running faster now, and I know why. The train's horn blaring in the distance reminds me why we're sprinting through the scorching savannah deprived of food, water, and sleep. We need to catch the train so we can get to the next town faster. It's the only way to save Soren in his current state.

My mask shows me the probabilities of future realities, as blue vector lines rise and expand within my aura field. I see the plain and simple future of us keeping our pace and reaching the train before it's gone. My aura field makes a whooshing sound and lines wriggle and snap suddenly like a snake striking. The vast blue space darkens, shrinks, and turns red, and my voice lurches from my throat to call Soren's name. As if on cue, my brother snarls and slows, throwing his hands up and collapsing to his knees.

"Soren!" I'm standing beside him the next moment, my chest tense with pain as I try to breathe.

He looks up at me with his bear mask on. With his holoskin activated, I see the byproduct of human and beast united, a distinct bear face on a burly human body. I used to be able to see Soren's eyes behind the mask, but now he's all bear. It's like he's losing himself to the mask and its power. He clutches his chest with his gauntlets, his bear claws tearing his shirt as he grimaces in silent pain. I kneel next to him then immediately jump up. The ground is too hot. Our masks must be pinching at our neurons and their effectiveness because my vision blurs, and it feels like my entire aura field is going to capsize.

I pull off my mask and hold my stomach as the outside world greets me in a dizzying rush of reds and browns. I take deep breaths, sucking in as much oxygen as I can. Soren's mask is off, and he's doing the same as he clutches the ground.

"Soren," I say, my voice barely a whisper. "We need food. Water."

Soren says nothing, and it takes me a moment to realize that he's crying. Tears stream down his face silently as he clenches his teeth.

"I'll kill him," Soren says.

"Hey." I put my hand on my brother's back, which is pooling with sweat and making his clothes cling to him. "You already did. You killed Dr. Fitz and saved us. We have to keep moving though." Even though I know we do, the red spot in my aura field gave me pause. And Soren collapsed a moment later.

"I'll kill 'em. Kill 'em all. That rat man and all his little rat friends," Soren says, his dried tears now turned to anger.

"Can you move? Can you get to that train with me?" I ask, pointing. I trace a path from the front of the train to the back, calculating how far away we are, the speed we'd need to reach it, how much time we'd have to get there before we're left to burn alive in the sun.

Soren sighs, slumping into me. "What do ya think he did to my mask?" His speech is slurred and slow. "I don't think I should wear it any ... anymore."

I shake my head and push air through my nostrils, swallowing more of my fear. I don't know how we're going to make it to the train. My throat tightens in that same way it does when something big and tragic is about to happen and I really don't want it to. That's when Dr. Fitz's rat mask falls out of my shirt where I tucked it after defeating him. I can almost see his cold, hollow eyes staring back at me, and I can't shake the image of his memory.

Then I break. "Why did you have to kill him?" I ask through tears that do not seem like mine. My body trembles, afraid of something I cannot see. "How are we supposed to know what he did? How am I supposed to help you?"

Soren gazes up at me as he turns his head. "Bro, I don't think you're going to figure this one out."

I grab Soren's bear claw hanging from his belt and use it to cut my pants above the knees, ripping the fabric in two. My mind is working quicker than my body, speeding me toward a solution that keeps our new collection of masks more secure. I tie my now loose pant legs together to create a satchel and put the rat mask inside, then I hook it to the holster on my back that holds my gem staff in place.

"Don't say that," I say. "Get up. We're not stopping here." I adjust Soren onto my shoulder and slowly stand, only a fraction of his weight against me.

"If I could take it back, I would," Soren says. I've never heard him so weak and defeated. "But then you might be dead."

A whirring sound, like the beating of grasshopper wings, grows louder in my ears. At first I think it is the train, its own organix activating and recycling the coal used to power the giant vessel along the tracks.

Then I see something resembling a miniature dark star hurtling across the savannah, a sphere of indestructible light glowing as it speeds toward us. I should probably be more worried about the unidentified object torpedoing in our direction, but I'm too exhausted to be scared, and besides there isn't time to do anything. The whirring gets louder as the darkened blur outlined in yellow light slows down in front of us. The figure, a boy close to my age, glides to a stop as though he's surfing on air, then hops down onto the ground from some kind of floating board.

The heat makes my thoughts and movements feel slower.

The boy brushes his fingers through his tousled brown hair, revealing yellow eyes as piercing as sunlight as he collects his breath. Tall and lean, he wears an oversized t-shirt and long pants that drape over his lithe frame.

"Who are you? Where did you even come from?" I ask, wondering if the extreme heat has made me delirious.

"Look at you guys," the boy says, flashing us a huge grin. His teeth are big and white, and his face is long like a horse's. Snatching his floating board out of midair, he tucks it under his arm. "What are you doing out here?"

It takes a moment for the question to reach me and for me to realize he completely ignored my questions. I hesitate. Something keeps me from speaking. I'd told Dr. Fitz things and he ended up using the data we fed him against us. I'm tired and not sure I could talk even if I wanted to.

He must notice.

"Here, have some gulpers." He reaches into his pack then holds out his hand, revealing small energy packets.

"Glupacs," I say, finding my voice.

Soren doesn't hesitate. He grabs a handful, leaving some for me.

I grab my share, rip one open and let the sugary, oozy goodness flood my mouth and tongue. Glupacs provide pure glucose and take up little room in a pack, making them useful for survival. I make a note to stock up on them when we can.

"Thank you," I say, before squeezing a second chocolate-vanilla pack down my throat.

"We gotta get to that train, guy," Soren says.

"You guys get into a fight?"

Of course our masks are showing. Soren is clutching his in his hand, and mine is tucked into the belt loop of my pants and covered partially by my shirt. Between running full speed to catch the train, and doing everything I can to save my brother, I had no time to hide our masks. The boy doesn't seem to notice or care in any way about the lynx or the bear, but his eyes do gleam at the presence of my gem staff and Soren's spiked club.

Time ticks by, and my worry for Soren grows. Color is returning to his pale face, but he might also just be sunburned.

"Something like that," I say. "What are you doing out here?"

The boy's eyes linger on Soren before he answers me. "I'm going to Oajin. Getting some use out of my hoverboard while I do. You guys are going to die out here if you don't catch that train. Next one isn't for another few hours. I have a spare board," the boy says, pulling a smaller board from the pack on his back. He presses a button in the center of the glowing device and it extends to a length matching the other one, a standard five feet. "You guys should take it."

"That isn't going to hold me," Soren says, and I'm inclined to agree.

"You're probably right," the boy says. "But I just charged it. You could try it."

Soren and I exchange glances. My brother is fading fast in this heat.

"If you don't want my help, let me know—I'll keep moving along. This heat makes me want to climb into an ice bath, and I have to get to Oajin by sundown. The train will be heading there. We can go together."

Soren steps forward, and the boy's eyes grow wider, fixed on Soren's club.

"I'm Benji, and this is Soren," I say.

"I'm Daniil," the boy says, shaking our hands. "Good to meet you guys."

I just want to get Soren to safety. "You too," I say.

The train horn blares again in the distance.

"We don't have much choice here, so I guess we'll fly," Soren says. "Thanks."

"We just need a ride to the train," I say, now wary of strangers who want to help us.

"Suit yourself. Do you know how to work them?"

Soren and I shake our heads. "It's organix?" I ask.

The boy nods. "Yeah, they're solar-powered."

"Why do you have two?" Soren asks.

"When one loses its charge, I have a spare," the boy says. He cocks his head, then gives us a short explanation of how to board them and use our weight to lean and choose a direction. I stand at the front of the board, and Soren stands behind me holding my shoulders.

"When you're ready, just tap that square behind your left foot three times, and it'll take flight." Daniil grins, then kicks off and is speeding away, a sphere of light once again.

With my boot, I tap the holosquare three times and our board wobbles as it rises. Our weight strains the board, but it still lifts us three feet off the ground. Soren squeezes my shoulders, and I know it's time to go.

So we go, a sweaty, heavy ball of light zooming into another unknown situation.

TWO

S oren and I are leaning forward to increase our speed, and I feel out of control, like any one move could be our last. Neither of us is wearing our masks, so a fall from this height at this speed would definitely mess us up. And we've been messed up enough the past two days. It's hard to believe that our final fight in the gauntlet was just yesterday, but time flies when you're having fun.

My stomach groans, starved for food. Now that it's had a taste, it wants more. The glupacs provided a small amount of electrolytes and hydration, but our bodies need more.

Soren's grip lightens on my shoulder.

I don't know how much longer we can stay on this board without passing out.

The train is close. I don't know what we're supposed to do now, but it doesn't matter because Daniil comes up beside us out of nowhere. Wind rushes past us, the dry air somewhat bearable as we speed toward the steel vessel. The 4-axle cars hum along the track, wheels sparking a neon green as the organix propels the hunk of metal forward. I look to Daniil for what to do next.

He glides close enough for us to touch, then hands me some kind of metal disc. With his eyes, and a quick jerk of his head, he gestures to us his next plan of action. I look at the disc for only a moment before Daniil airsurfs away, zipping toward the glint of moving train, a flash of yellow light. We're about three quarters of the way down the train's silver body when we finally reach it as it moves across the savannah at what must be one-hundred miles per hour.

Daniil dips forward toward the train, and it looks like he will crash into it, but he holds up the disc, creating a magnetic connection. Then he seems to relax, no longer leaning forward or controlling his hoverboard actively.

He's linked himself to the train and is using its energy to ride forward.

Soren mumbles something in my ear, but the wind is too loud for me to hear him. I can feel him fading. If he passes out and falls, it could kill him.

In my delirium, I copy Daniil's movements as he waves us on with his other hand. I approach and reach out with disc in hand. The magnetic force yanks me forward and connects me invisibly to the moving train. Soren's grip tightens on my shoulders and we stabilize.

This is wild. I never thought I'd be riding a hoverboard or airsurfing along a moving train. The lights on our hoverboard soften, powering down by one degree. Daniil is ahead of us, and the landscape looks totally different now as I look back to where we just came from. We were able to cover serious ground with the hoverboards. The savannah is a canvas of burnt orange and amber, like a painting slicked in oily light. I can just barely see the river snake out of view beyond the canyon, the last place we saw Dr. Fitz.

I turn to my brother as wind whips the hair on our heads everywhere. There are purple rings under his sunken eyes. "We need more food," I shout above the soft hum of the wheels below us. "And water."

Soren nods, his eyes closing.

Daniil is beside us again. He must have released his disc and slid down the train's body to be near us.

"We're not doing so good," I tell Daniil.

He must already know because he nods toward the end of the train. "We can get in there," he says, projecting his voice, boyish but on the verge of manhood.

"How?" I look at the disc, a strange fear that I might lose control building inside me.

Daniil stares at his hand then at me and shouts, "Unflex your fingers this way. Away from your palm to release."

I hate that I have to trust someone new and am at the mercy of yet another stranger. But Daniil seems genuine and like he wants to help us. Besides, he seems just like us, not some cranky old doctor living in the sewers who faked his own death.

Our eyes meet. "Like this," Daniil says, and he performs his little release trick again, pushing himself away from the train as he glides down to the caboose.

"Give it to me," Soren says, his own voice gruff, his amber eyes fiery and stark in the morning light.

Soren is technically a weapons master of sorts, but changing hands seems risky at this speed. I know o-tech and organix just as well, and the disc is no different than any magnetic device or mechanism I've handled.

I unflex my fingers away from my palm, feeling a sudden jolt as Soren curses under his breath. Our connection weakens. The train speeds on as we glide down toward the end, toward Daniil. We're backward, and I don't have the skill to turn our board.

"Lean forward!" Soren shouts.

I know he's right. We're moving too fast in the other direction. Soren's weight presses against me, almost knocking me off. In the corner of my eye, I see Daniil's outstretched hand as we clear the end of the train. I grab it. Our bodies jerk again, my shoulder nearly ripping from its socket, and I almost flip backward off the board. There's a second jolt, and I see that Soren has grabbed a railing and is pulling us onto the caboose. Daniil helps us board.

We all take a moment to catch our breath and stand on our feet. The wind shrieks in my ears. I scoop up the hoverboard, holding the long, sturdy piece of tech under my arm. Daniil and I share a quick smile, but Soren just shakes his head in disbelief. Without waiting for a plan of action, he grabs the train's door and yanks it open. Daniil and I follow.

I have never been inside a train before, but it looks like what I imagined. Compartments on both sides. Cool grey metal under our feet. Mint green trim decorates the rims around the doors. Daniil presses his ear against the first door we come across, then opens it. There is no one inside. He steps in and motions for us to follow.

"Soren," I hiss, but he's bounding forward in blind angst.

"Not now," he says. "Need food."

Daniil shrugs and sits down in the compartment. I watch Soren for a moment, then sit across from Daniil, needing a moment to catch my breath and cool down. Daniil isn't fazed at all. Inside the compartment, I feel how out of place we are, how big and cumbersome everything I'm carrying with me is.

"Here," I say, holding the board out for Daniil. "You can have this back. Thank you for saving us … from the heat," I finish awkwardly.

Daniil clears a tussled mess of sweaty hair from his face, smiling wide as he takes the board back. "Don't mention it. The capital is nuts right now. I was going home anyway." He presses a button on his board, and it slowly shrinks inside itself, collapsing into a smaller version of its original state. He does it to his second one, then leans them up against the wall.

My gem staff presses into my back, where it's been tucked away, but I'm suddenly aware of how out of place I must be with such a large, uncommon weapon. The weapon of the lynx. Anyone with two brain cells who saw the gauntlet could figure out who I am, though, since I'm not wearing my mask, it is only half its full size. I think of Soren and his gauntlets, the bear claws on the end of them, how they grow three times their original size once his mask is on. Footsteps thump outside, so I slide our door open to look down the train's hallway but see no one.

"You okay, man? You seem rattled," Daniil says. His eyes scan me up and down, and I know he's stopped on my staff. He's probably seen my mask sticking out too.

I don't give them attention. "Yeah, just worried about my brother. What's going on in the capital?"

Daniil's eyes grow wide. "Riots. People are rebelling against the Crown. The Fall Gauntlet ended in chaos." He opens the curtain and the outside world showers our compartment in golden sunlight. The boards, which are now half their size at two-and-a-half feet in length, respond to the light like a flower reaching toward the sun, opening to its power. Green lights flicker on one by one, slowly, like a train going around a track. Daniil sees me watching. "They need sun."

"How did you get them?" I ask, watching this boy with new interest. I've had very little interaction with boys my own age since my family was separated, and I'm surprised at how I've never thought about it, or fully realized it until this very moment.

"I made them," Daniil says, beaming. Now that I have a second to breathe, I notice how tanned Daniil is. His face and arms are bronzed, probably from so much time on his boards in the sun, but I recognize it must be genetic to an extent too. His arms, veiled in a light layer of dark hair, contrast with his smooth face. "A guy has gotta make his own way, ya know? Your brother and you seem to get that. Guys like us can stick together."

Daniil is thin and wiry like me, but there's something about him that seems more experienced. Probably because the Crown never put him on house arrest.

"Yeah," I say, my heart thumping faster in my chest.

I don't know what to say after that.

I have so many questions about everything that I don't know the first question to ask. I want to know what's happening in the capital, what will happen now that the Fall Gauntlet is over, or postponed, or starting anew, or whatever the hell is happening from the aftermath of Soren's and my decision to escape the gauntlet together. I want to know if other boys and girls are out there making weapons and ciantech and cool hoverboards that give them the ability to fly through the air. I want to know more about Daniil too, but I'm interrupted by an even louder rumble that echoes down the hallway: Soren's voice.

I'm out of the compartment the next moment, striding down the hallway toward Soren.

He's on his knees at someone else's half-open compartment door. A young girl peeks her head out, her hair and features dark. She's smiling down at Soren with kind eyes.

"Did you need something else?" she asks.

Other compartment doors are open, and people are watching the bear of a man that is Soren as he tries to stand on his feet.

I'm beside him the next moment, pulling him up underneath the arms, but he's dead weight. The girl's face swims into view and I'm face-to-face with her. She shoots me a sharp look. "Is he *okay*?"

"Not feeling so good," Soren says. "Need to lie down."

The girl smiles thinly. "I gave him some of my macarons. He didn't have any money. Do you know him?"

"He's my brother," I say, trying to pull him up, but failing. "Soren, let's get you to the compartment."

Soren is creating quite the commotion, and now even more people are out of their compartments, their eyes glued to us.

"Tickets," a man says right in my ear.

I turn to see a young man dressed in white pants and blue collared shirt. Behind him, Daniil watches us from the last compartment.

I try to get Soren up. There's no way we're getting kicked off this train. The girl must see the desperation in my eyes as I look to her because she says, "They're with me, sir."

"Show me your tickets," the man says. "And please get inside your compartment. You must stay inside your compartment while the train is in motion unless going to the bathroom or food station."

The girl does something quick to her wrist, some kind of ciantech device that blinks and flashes in the late morning light. She holds it out and the man presses two fingers to the interface on the inside of her wrist.

"One, two, three," he says, each number its own separate beep. "Good, now please get inside your compartment, or I will have to remove you from the train." He's all business and no pleasure, and I definitely don't want any more trouble at this stage in our journey, so I pull Soren up with more strength than I've had all day, and he budges, staggering to his feet, then launching himself onto one of the seats in the girl's compartment.

"I'm going to throw up," Soren says, and I believe him.

Everything happens quickly from there.

I study the girl who covered for us. She's somewhere between laughing at my brother's shenanigans and fearful of what trouble this new human may bring to the rest of her train ride. She pulls something from her pocket, and the unmistakable scent of lavender fills the compartment. She wafts some kind of bottle underneath Soren's nostrils, and he relaxes as he draws longer, deeper breaths.

I don't know how Daniil is here too, but he's somehow slipped into the compartment as well, making it even more cramped. Soren takes up the entire seat on one side, and the girl flops down on the other seat across from Soren with only one spot left next to her.

"Who are you?" the girl asks, looking up at Daniil with eyes that whorl with questions.

"I'm Daniil. Who are you?"

"I'm Lyaza," she says, capping her scented bottle and slipping it back in her pocket.

"I'm Benji and this is my brother—"

"Soren," Lyaza says, finishing my sentence. "We've met." Lyaza watches him and seems to be holding back a laugh.

Soren grins.

I wonder what happened when my brother met Lyaza, and how he seemed to acquire some of her macarons. I don't have time to think about it, and instead slump down in the seat next to Lyaza.

A moment of awkwardness fills the air as Daniil looks to the seat completely filled by Soren. Soren's eyes shift slowly, not bear-like, but reptilian, toward Daniil.

"This compartment seems full," Daniil says, his voice dropping an octave, the spark of joy gone from his eyes.

Now everyone seems to be looking at me.

I'm chewing on my lip, and my heart's a galloping stallion inside my chest. I feel like a rag doll being thrown around, but I know I need to say something and get this situation under control. "I'm going to stay with my brother for now, Daniil, but I'll—"

"Don't sweat it, Benji," he says, cutting me off. He tilts his head and narrows his eyes. "You and your brother take care of yourselves. Maybe I'll see you around."

"Daniil," I start, not sure if I've offended him, my thoughts bouncing around and spiraling, telling me that I'm selfish and using people, and fully out of control. I have more to say, but Daniil doesn't wait for any of it.

The compartment closes with a whoosh, and he's gone.

I sigh deeply, as a storm of emotions rushes out of me in a jet stream.

"And my grandma says my sister and I are sensitive," Lyaza says with a sly grin.

"What?" I turn to look at this new person who seems to have saved us from getting kicked off the train. And who fed my dying brother.

"Oh nothing," she says. "You guys don't look so hot." She pauses as she gazes out into the hot bare savannah, whirling by in an auburn blur. "And you smell terrible." A giggle escapes her lips. "Don't worry so much about other people," she says. "Like that boy's feelings."

My eyes are on the door again. "Why'd you help us?"

Lyaza is silent for a moment. "I'm a people person, and I know when someone needs me, I guess. That boy wasn't going to be any more help to you, only trouble." She looks me up and down, like she knows something.

"What do you mean?" My attention is fully back with her now.

"I mean that he knows exactly who you are, and he was ready to take advantage of you," Lyaza says in her sweet, girlish lilt.

At first I wonder if Soren talked, but before I can protest, she says, "You really ought to hide your staff and bear claws better. People like Daniil and me can quickly figure out you're bear and lynx supporters, which isn't the cutest thing to be right now by the way, but you don't need everyone in the whole wide world knowing."

I stare at her, unblinking. I'm about to say something, but I'm so tired, and my brain doesn't seem to be working.

And anyway, whatever I say won't be heard. We're drowned out by Soren's sudden snoring.

THREE

I wake to the sound of feet pattering and doors whooshing open. I'm in a dark dreamscape, and then I'm not, my eyes opening and assaulted by dazzling sunlight and seas of color streaming past our compartment door like a river. I draw a sharp breath into my lungs.

"Wake up sleepyheads," says a familiar voice. Lyaza swims into view, her dark lashes flickering as she grins and readjusts her backpack, her black hair flipping about.

"Shoot," I mumble. "I fell asleep." Fatigue and soreness ripple through me as consciousness returns, each cut and bruise making itself known.

Lyaza moves toward the door, revealing Soren still asleep behind her. He's curled up with one leg hanging over the seat's edge. His hands are nestled under his head like a pillow.

"Where are we?" I ask, yanking on my boots, which I must have loosened and taken off in my delirium before falling asleep. My breath is sticky and hot and everything on me has the unwelcome smell of old sweat and body odor.

"Oajin," Lyaza says. "Oasis of the desert. This is home. The spa I run with my sister is called Chi Spa." Lyaza pauses, her eyes shifting back and forth between Soren and me, then lighting up. "Hey, why don't you guys come to Chi Spa with me? You both need a bath. And new clothes. And probably several other things that I don't have time to list."

I stand. "Why are you being so nice to us?" Why indeed. Why did Daniil help us? People can just be nice and helpful. I think of the bronzed boy with the horseface and big nose, so much more comfortable in his body than I am. I want to be traveling with him, not Lyaza. I'm annoyed that I fell asleep because he's probably long gone now.

"My sister and I need help around the spa," Lyaza says. "We could use you and Soren for a few days while you recover and get your bearings. It's a win for both of us." She offers a thin smile.

"Thank you, Lyaza." Mom always used people's names even after she had just met them. She said it made remembering the name easier. Something told me I wouldn't be forgetting Lyaza anytime soon. "I need to get Soren better first."

"Is he sick?" Lyaza cranes toward us, balancing on her toes.

I don't answer her question. "Is there a good doctor around?"

"Dr. Yune is good," Lyaza says. He's old, though." She pauses, sizing us up. "Don't you know that a spa is even better than a doctor?"

I shake Soren awake. He's been out cold, and my worry for him returns as his eyes slowly open. "C'mon, bro. Get up. We need to get you some help."

Soren awakens like a bear stirring from hibernation. He sets his feet on the floor, his boots still strapped to his feet.

"That was weird. Did we ... stop in the forest somewhere?"

"I was asleep too, but pretty sure not even close. We're in the desert."

Soren wipes a thin layer of dirt and sweat from his face with his sleeve. "That felt so real."

"I'll call a tuk-tuk," Lyaza says. "C'mon, let's go."

Soren stands, but he's a bit shaky. "Where we going?"

"Lyaza's invited us back to her spa," I say.

"Here, use these." Lyaza tosses us pieces of fabric. "They'll be less conspicuous." She notices us staring at the basic beige fabric and says, "They're camo-sleeves. They can stretch up to six times their size. Put them over that monster of a club of yours, and that staff, which clearly has a very rare jewel inside."

Camo-tech. Of course. It hid the chains used to hold up the Fall Gauntlet arena. Once I figured out the chains were there, Soren and I used them to escape.

I slide the fabric's open pouch over my staff to hide the gem. My staff just looks like a sturdy walking stick. Soren's club looks like it could be a bundle of kindling inside a beige sack.

"Okay, these are cool," Soren says.

"You're welcome. Now hurry up and keep up." Lyaza backs out of the doorway and then is gone, lost in the slow parade of people leaving the train.

"Are we going?" Soren asks.

"I don't know yet." I face Soren, our eyes meeting. "I need you to stall Lyaza a little bit while I figure something out."

Soren arches an eyebrow. "Why are you being mysterious? No secrets, bro. Figure what out?"

"I'm just trying to be careful," I say, barely above a whisper. "I need to put on my mask and get the lay of the land. See what our potential actions are."

"Oh, so you can put your mask on, but I can't?" Soren scoffs, but I can tell he's trying to get a rise out of me. The short nap has done wonders for him.

I grin. "We don't have much time. Can you cover me? It will only take a minute."

Soren claps me on the back, and I nearly fall into him. "You know I can. Go get us some answers you foxy lynx."

When I get off the train and step onto the boarding platform, warm air rushes to greet me. Soren strides ahead of me to catch up with Lyaza as the crowds of people thin out and head to the shelter of the train station. The train had vents that kept us cool, but now we're back in the desert air, and it's *hot*. Unbelievably hot. I hold up my hand to block the sun's glare. It's directly above us, telling me it's midday. We must have slept for at least two hours.

I climb the side of the train, my muscles aching from battle and so much movement. I'm quiet as I reach the top and am about to jump down off the other side so I can put the mask on without anyone seeing, but something catches my eye. I turn.

"Wow," is all I can say.

The mountains are cloaked in heavy layers of afternoon light. Everything is glowing. Each peak and plateau is its own shade of red, orange, beige, or brown. The cloudless sky is blue and endless, and the landscape is breathtaking.

I wasn't exposed to much nature in New Phasia, and I yearn to be in it now. After we save Mom, I decide, we're going to live wherever we want.

I remember myself and where I am and scramble down the train's other side, anxious I may have wasted too much time. Pulling my mask out from my belt loop, I press it to my face and undergo the usual pleasure-pain pendulum that swings once, twice, three times as I clench my stomach and push down the bile that wants to leave my body, and then it's over and I'm light, lithe, and lynx-like. Underneath the mask, I'm me, but outside I'm feline, commanding and fierce in presence. The fur at the end of my ears seems to reach new heights. My senses snap into hyperfocus.

I scan the vast desert before me, then look to the mountains and into town, through the sprawl of red-thatched roofs. I wait for something to be revealed. My steps are slow and careful as my aura field activates and washes the world blue then brightens once like a star dying, everything in front of me washed in glittering brilliance—

I hold on.

This is different.

A vortex of energy wraps me up like a cocoon. Step by step, I'm pulled to the mountains by steady gales of wind, like I'm underwater and the undertow is sucking me in.

Come to me. Please, come to me.

The words come from a strange voice I've never heard before, and it's as though the voice is whispering into my ear.

I leap on top of the train in one bound, then slink forward on all fours as if the lynx is in control, walking toward the voice, putting us in plain sight. I want to pull away, but I can't. Fascination and fear run through me, my adrenaline nearly bursting out of my veins as the sun glares down.

Come release me from these shackles.

The voice is deep and pained. It feels like someone—something is out there. Trapped? Forgotten? Alone? All those things. Information comes to me by way of the voice, by things that aren't being said. The lynx feels it. I feel it.

And I'm terrified.

Bright light flashes to my right like lightning, and the spell—whatever was holding me, calling me, is gone as I jerk away and pull my mask off my face. I can't explain the feeling because it's the first time I've felt it. It's like the lynx needed to be distracted for Benji to pull away.

Why does it feel like those two things are separate?

I'm sucking in much-needed oxygen, trying to stabilize myself from the voice's undeniable pull on me. Was that ... a deus? I don't have time to think about it more because the light is distracting me again.

I slip my mask inside another camo-sleeve and tuck it into my belt loop. Soft ambient lights emerge from the train station as though there is a holomovie on inside. It seems like everyone is in there. That explains why no one saw me.

I jump off the train and descend the steps, scurrying under the awning and into the station. My heart is thumping against my chest. People are scattered around. Voices buzz with mounting excitement. The station is airy and open, almost regal with ivory columns thirty feet high and as thick as oak trees. Propellor fans whirl within the ceiling's alcoves, pushing cool air down in great swaths.

I search for Soren and Lyaza. The raw, anticipatory energy coming from this mishmash of people is palpable. It feels like something is about to happen. I didn't see anyone outside but maybe there are more exits? No, they have to be in here. I slink and slide through the crowds until I glimpse, from the corner of my eye, neon lights on a miniature board, drawing my gaze in like a magnet to a boy standing twenty feet away.

Daniil. Looks like he didn't get far either.

He glances my way and our eyes meet and hold, as though we both suddenly realized the other was there. He grins at me and waves. My heart beats faster and sweat drips from my palms. I feel bad for ditching him on the train, but he's smiling at me like nothing happened. When I catch my breath, I notice he's pointing to the opposite wall where everyone is staring. Light flashes, and I now see what drew my gaze earlier—it *is* a holomovie.

It's being projected onto the wall, which is one giant digi-screen. The skylight above closes, blocking out the sun from above and enveloping us in an ominous darkness. Sunlight streams through the windows as lights dance with shadows.

"Daniil!" I say, brushing past people to get to him. He's holding one hoverboard under his arm and has the other attached to a holster on his back, and he's staring at the wall like everyone else. "Hey, what is this—"

"Watch," he says in a whisper, his eyes gleaming. The holomovie starts as I turn to face it. But it's not a holomovie. It's just words on a screen in neon bright text and another voice, sweet but monotone, echoing through the station.

>>Greetings, challenger …

>>The hour of the condor approaches. Do you have what it takes to be the next chosen one? Find your way to central station's rooftop at the seventh evehour when the moon is full and bright to speak your sacrifice to the Dei. They will decide which of you is worthy to carry on their will. They will decide which of you shall become the condor.

>>May you fly far and with the grace of a sky-born

>>The Fall Gauntlet continues …

The screen goes black, casting us in darkness, and it's like I'm back in the gauntlet tunnels. A yellow light flashes, like the sun's first ray in the morning, and a mask—one I've never seen before—drifts into view. An ugly-looking bird with a devastating beak and tribal patterns resting above its eyes stares back at me.

Condor.

"What does it mean, 'the Fall Gauntlet continues'?" Soren asks as the digitized condor mask fades from view and the room grows bright again. He appears out of nowhere. "The Fall Gauntlet clearly ended ... yesterday."

"Apparently not," Daniil says above the excited and growing chatter. "Did you come to speak your sacrifice to the Dei?" He flashes a toothy grin. I can't tell if he's joking or not.

"The hour of the condor," I repeat. "Do totem ceremonies happen outside the capital?"

"Of course," Daniil says. "The gods and goddesses want to attract talent from all over the land, not just the capital. Some people don't have the money or means to travel to the capital, so there are always other ceremonies elsewhere."

It wasn't even something I had considered. I figured all the fighters found different temples and holy homes within the capital but apparently I'm sheltered, even when it comes to the Fall Gauntlet. That's what happens when you serve under the Crown, I suppose.

"Besides," Daniil continues. "It didn't end. The final fighters fled the scene apparently. Young guys, wearing bear and lynx masks. It's been all over the digi-casts. No one got a good look at their faces, and the identities of the fighters can't be revealed so I think the Crown is staying pretty tight-lipped about it."

Could that be true? Could no one have seen our faces? We were masked most of the time, and the stadium itself sits back several hundred feet or so from the arena. But then, Dr. Fitz knew who we were.

But not at first.

Does Lyaza know?

She could have inferred it from our weapons, but she called us lynx and bear "supporters." She did give us camo-sleeves though, which meant she was trying to hide us, or have us hide ourselves. Is she playing us? It's fairly clear that Daniil doesn't know much about what happened either and seems to be clueless about our weapons.

"You guys want to come back and see what it's all about?" he asks. "It's a few days away."

Soren doesn't miss a beat. "And get murdered by someone desperate enough to risk their life for the promise of a single wish? No, thank you!"

Daniil laughs. "I'm not going to enter. I like my life too much, but I want to see how it works. Aren't you curious? The mask only chooses one person. It could be anyone here. The masks use ciantech and other ancient tech that's said to be passed down from the Dei."

"If you aren't going to enter, why waste your time?" Soren asks.

"Because I want to be part of something. I never believed in any of the totem animals, and maybe that's why I've never found my tribe. It's not a good time to be a loner with everything going on. And the condor is pretty cool." He pauses, then releases a soft sigh. "I wouldn't mind learning to fly with the grace of a sky-born."

Is this the tribe Daniil means? A bunch of strangers coming together to become one with the condor, and all others following behind faithfully? Fatefully?

"Right," Soren says, his voice almost mocking. "Anyway, I came to get you, Benji. I need food and Lyaza is ready to go. Wrap it up." He pulls at my arm, then stalks off alone.

"We can practice more on these later," Daniil says, patting his board.

I try to process all the information that has been thrust upon me over the last few hours. People are dispersing, leaving the train station in groups or pairs. It's now making sense to me how and why people took the train here.

So they can have their wish granted.

I remember feeling excitement and hunger for that power, one that has never been yours before but can be. All you had to do was be chosen.

Daniil mentioned the Dei and I'm thinking about the gods and goddesses that are said to bestow upon our planet Calypso prosperity and peace, but all I see is chaos and ruin. How can the Dei watch their world fall apart as brothers fight to the death to destroy each other?

"Do you think you're the only one looking to save someone?" Master Gherus had asked.

The capital is rioting. Mom and Dad are still captive, if in fact still alive, and the Fall Gauntlet continues.

That last one is the kicker because it means that Soren and I are being hunted, essentially.

This is bad. This is really bad.

"I can't."

Daniil is startled. "Hey, you okay, Benji?"

I look at him, stunned, his eyes wide, my eyes wide, and I realize that I may have screamed at him.

"Sorry," I say, meeting his gaze. My heart is a jackrabbit hammering in my chest again. I'm anxious about what I'm going to say next. "I'm sorry, but I can't. Not right now. Things are ... confusing right now." I don't want to tell him my feelings, but the words spill out of me. "I do want to practice more, but I need food, water, and sleep. It's been a long day. How can I find you?"

He laughs and smirks, then claps me on the chest in a brotherly sort of way. "I'll be around. Oajin isn't big. Take care, man."

"Thanks for everything," I say, turning on my heel and darting outside. My chest aches as I realize I want to be his friend, but I can't add complications to my life right now.

"Hurry up," Soren says. He and Lyaza are sitting inside a tuk-tuk. There's an open seat next to the driver. He sees me and waves.

"Soren, come on. We need to talk," I say. "Lyaza, sorry we can't go with you."

"The hell we can't," Soren says, his eyes wide and unbelieving. He's gotten some of his life back—probably because he can smell the food from here. "Are you coming or not? Lyaza has hot baths and healing hands. What do you have except smelly boots?"

I'd laugh if I weren't so scared for our lives.

"I'll make it easy for you, big bro," Soren says, his eyes unblinking, his jaw clenched in tired frustration. "You can either come with Lyaza and me back to the spa, or you can stay here with your new friend."

If he's thinking of Lyaza as a friend, I'll be sure to shake that idea loose from his head. We aren't here to make friends or trust people. Not until we know what people want. Everybody in this world wants something, and I won't let my naivete get us into trouble again. I have to be the bigger brother and take care of us.

"Fine," I say, taking a seat next to the driver. "Let's go get cleaned up."

"You can thank me later," Lyaza says, as the driver hits the gas and the tuk-tuk wheels away, spitting up pebbles and sand. "Like I said, there's plenty of work to do around the spa, and you boys look so *strong.*"

I roll my eyes. Turning my head, I glance back at the train station and see Daniil emerge, his hoverboard in hand. He hops onto it like the air is water and he's surfing the waves and then speeds away, past us and over the barren dunes to our right.

Gherus always said distractions get you killed. I face the road, smelling the smoky air. He hasn't been wrong so far.

FOUR

We pull up to Chi Spa some twenty minutes later to Soren complaining about not having enough food. My own stomach growls, aching for sustenance, while thirst claws at my throat.

I stagger out of the tuk-tuk, my legs weary, while Lyaza settles payment with a tap of her card. The stone path leading to the spa is worn. Statues of birds, amphibians, and reptiles are scattered across the porch. Cacti of different bulbous and spiked shapes create a desert garden around the perimeter. I instinctively reach for my mask, but I catch myself and play it off, like I'm brushing dirt off my shirt. Part of me wants to hear more from that voice. I need to tell Soren what I heard.

When I look at him, he's completely still, peering up at the spa, at the promise of food and rest. So close. And yet—Soren is fighting something. He grimaces and puts a hand to his stomach. Glimpses of us in the sewers return to me, of when Dr. Fitz turned Soren against me by doing something to his mask. How he fell to his knees. How a stranger could turn him into someone else.

Soren shakes his head, inhales sharply, then hurries up the steps to the spa.

Lyaza takes a slower pace and says, "You don't have to tell me what happened to him, but it might help us a lot more if you do."

Inside, the wooden floors glow as the final rays of sunlight stream through the windows. Massage tables sit behind translucent paper screens. The space is bare and simple, all end tables, ottomans for propping up feet to wash them, and a laundry basket filled with white towels. Relaxing scents float through the air, which I guess must be different massage oils, none of which I can identify.

"I don't care what you make us do here, just please show me where the food is," Soren says, his tone desperate. "I won't last long."

"When's the last time you guys ate?" Lyaza asks. "He was like this on the train too." She looks up at me, and I realize how short she is, at least a foot shorter than me, but then again she looks much younger too, younger than Soren by a year or two, I'd guess.

"I told you," I say. "He's sick. He needs something for his fever."

"Miki!" Lyaza shouts in the direction of the rooms upstairs. To us, she adds, "You two can eat once you wash up. Those are the rules."

A girl emerges from one of the upper rooms and takes care to close the sliding door behind her. She descends the sturdy wooden steps and approaches us, her thick slippers shuffling across the floor.

"Who do we have here?" the older girl asks.

"I met them on the train," Lyaza says. "This one's sick. Can we help him?"

Miki passes me without even a second glance to inspect my brother. Soren looks down at her like a lumbering beast, his breath shallow and pupils dilated. Miki's dark eyes narrow, and her heartbeat quickens noticeably, her small frame expanding like lungs in distress. "Steam room. Some chrystea. And some rest." Miki claps, summoning two attendants in beige robes, who move with surprising swiftness. They escort Soren to a different room with some effort, leaving me with Lyaza and—

"I'm Michaela," Miki says. "Call me Miki. And you are?"

"I'm Benji," I say. "That was my brother, Soren."

"Are you warriors? Ready to take down the Crown like everyone else?" She fixes her gaze on my "walking stick" and Soren's club, which has slipped out of its camo-sleeve and is lying in the middle of the floor, flecked with dried blood.

"Well—" I begin, not sure which lie to feed Miki. Both girls are direct. Definitely sisters. "We're going to see my uncle out west. We fled the capital after the craziness with the gauntlet—"

"Savagery," Miki says, and her eyes reflect the sun's relentless fire through the mostly closed blinds. "The Harvest cycle ended, and there's no champion. I don't think anyone realizes how bad things are going to get." Her voice is loud, commanding, charismatic.

"What do you mean?" I know about the Fall Gauntlet continuing and the Crown recruiting new champions, but I hadn't fully considered the implications of what would happen with Harvest. I added, "It's not like the gods and goddesses are actually going to do anything."

Miki's eyes darken, and I see a storm of blind rage brew and crackle before me. "What did you just say?"

"I mean …" I don't want to say the wrong thing again. "They haven't been around for millennia. What will they do?"

Lyaza is standing by idly, watching her sister in half-trepidation, half-admiration. Miki sighs. "They don't need to show themselves to the likes of us. We are peasants to them."

"Even the champions?" I ask. "They are the Dei's chosen vessels and determine the Harvest cycle."

Miki drops her shoulders and cocks her head to the side, sizing me up like Lyaza had done hours before. "Yes, the champion is important. Crucial to our survival. Those brothers screwed everything up, and now we're all going to pay."

I don't know how or why it happens, but as if on cue, the weather responds to our conversation. At first it sounds like nails dropping onto the roof. Then it comes faster, deadlier, like tiny needles stabbing the roof. The sky opens up, offering all its dark secrets, and it feels like too much for this little wooden spa. The rain sloshes down in sheets and lightning cracks, ripping the oncoming night sky in two. I cover my ears.

"See, they're already here." Miki's eyes widen, taking in the gravity of her own statement.

"What do we do?" I ask, truly needing to know.

"We do what we've always done," Miki says, as she takes long slow breaths, falling into a more balanced state with the rain. "We appeal to them, offer ourselves and our penance. Just like the Fall Gauntlet but in a different way." Miki looks at Lyaza and nods, and they share an exchange that is lost on me. "Since it's raining, have him use the indoor bathtub, then put them in the guest room upstairs. We're closed for a few days for renovations."

"Yes, sister." Lyaza's tone is sweet, but her grin tells another story.

The bath is one of the most magnificent experiences I've had in my life. The water is warm and the copper tub is soothing to my sore muscles. I take my time as I scrub a handheld saltbomb across my wounds, scraping dried blood, clumps of dirt, and dead skin off my body. Salt crystals flake off with each pass.

I bite into my lower lip, trying to withstand the pain.

With each push and pull of the bomb to cleanse myself, residual pain rings through my bones. I find it funny. Maybe a little bit twisted. Even when the fight is over, the pain still lives inside you until you find a way to push it out.

Master Gherus had a bath in the outhouse that I used when the solar-powered shower was being repaired, but the water was always cold, a deeply unpleasant experience in the winter. I don't love the sweltering heat of the desert, but there is something purifying about it. Something that makes me want to forget my troubles and melt into myself.

I clean myself this way for a while, inspecting each open wound on my knees, elbows, arms, and legs. My fights versus Soren and then Dr. Fitz left me relatively unscathed, but I know they won't all be that way. Both battles were more cerebral than any I've fought, games of wit and gaining an advantage through words and just the right amount of force when the time called for it.

The electric attack.

I'd thought about it at the time, when a bolt of electricity left my gem staff and struck Dr. Fitz right in the chest, but everything has happened so fast since then that I haven't had time to think about it.

Why did my staff generate an electric ... bolt? Blast? Ray?

I know it can create centrifugal force the longer I build up kinetic energy, but I had no idea it could act as a projectile weapon, much less conjure electricity.

Then I remember what I did and *why* I did it.

My mask had shown me the probability of me whirling my staff above my head. The action that followed was immediate. I did it and the next thing I knew, Dr. Fitz was chock-full of electricity, and I was holding him up by the neck as electrical currents zipped through his body. My own fight-not-flight adrenaline and my gauntlet had momentarily lessened the electricity's effects when I grabbed him. I was so intent on saving Soren that nothing else seemed to matter. Or hurt.

It was like the mask, and the things that came with it— the gauntlet and the gem staff—protected me. They made me more powerful than I've ever been. Then there was what Soren did when he sent Dr. Fitz flying off the edge. The tip of Dr. Fitz's needle gleamed in the early morning sun as he fell to his death.

I remind myself that all of that happened this morning.

There were still so many things to discuss and figure out, and I needed Soren for all of them. I finish scrubbing myself with the saltbomb, wearing it away to the size of a pebble, then take the wad of seaweed that Lyaza gave me and rub it all over my body. It stings terribly. Minerals and vitamins seep into my raw, open pores, creating a strange new kind of pain. One that is not rough but lingers, like my body's been sprayed with an oral mint freshener from the inside-out.

I get out of the bath and start to dry off when I hear a knock. I'm too slow, too preoccupied to realize that the knock is for me.

After a few seconds, Lyaza enters the bathroom, this now steamy sanctuary of ivory, marble, and copper.

I scramble to get the towel on the rack but am not fast enough. Embarrassment flushes my cheeks as I snatch the towel, then wrap it around my waist. I don't think my body can get any hotter than it is now.

"Benji, sorry. I couldn't wait," Lyaza says. "You've been in here awhile. I need to use it. Here's the key to your room upstairs. Soren is sleeping in the room next to yours. Don't wake him. He's running a fever."

I'm taking in all this information as I recover from Lyaza just seeing all my parts, dripping with water and burning with residual pain. "Is he going to be okay?"

"I don't know. There's something psychosomatic happening."

"Like ... some traumatic event that's manifesting as physical pain?"

"You aren't as slow as you look," Lyaza says. "I need to know more, but it seems like you and your brother don't want to tell me what actually happened, so it's hard to be helpful."

I consider this. "We lost our mother a few years ago, and my father too. Soren was young, and it happened in a bad way. I think it's still traumatic for him. He hasn't fully processed it, or dealt with it, I think."

"I see," Lyaza says, her eyes crinkling.

Empathy?

"That's something we have in common."

I stop drying my lower half and look at Lyaza.

She's looking down, frowning. "The Crown took our parents away too. Ever since that happened, Miki's been obsessed with the Dei, trying to commune with them, find them, learn everything she can about them. She thinks that the gauntlet works for what we're trying to do, but she also feels its outdated and not what the gods and goddesses truly want. She believes there's a way to commune with the Dei more directly."

"More ... directly?" I ask, stunned.

Lyaza sighs and purses her lips. "Have you ever heard of the Fallen Goddess?"

"No. What's that?"

"It's a long story actually, and I need to bathe. I'll have to tell you later." Lyaza's soft demeanor hardens and she walks past me to the bathtub, unplugging the drain. "I'll take it from here, let's talk later."

I hurry out of the bathroom without another word, darting for my upstairs bedroom with my clothes bundled against my chest. I don't need to be wearing my lynx mask to know that Lyaza is holding back a lot of pain.

Once I'm dressed in the robe laid out for me, which seems to be the garb for after sunset around here, I eat the meal that's been set aside for me: a bowl of steamed vegetables and rice, topped with seaweed. Then I pay Soren a visit. The room is dark, except for a tealight at the head of his bed, which is just a mattress on the floor.

His breaths are long and deep. Fear grips me because I don't know what they gave him or fed him. After the rat, I'm not taking chances.

"Soren?" I whisper. "There's so much we need to talk about. I really need you right now. I know you need rest. I should get some too. We'll talk when we've both had some."

Outside, rain lashes the windows, and the world becomes a vicious sea of grainy blue.

I should have talked to Soren when I had the chance. I should have pulled him aside as soon as I heard the voice talk to me. Leaving Soren to sleep, I return to my corner room and collapse onto the mattress on the floor. They've separated us, which means I can't keep an eye on Soren, but I'm too exhausted to do anything about it, and besides I can't. Sleep pulls me down into its endless shaft of darkness.

Here we are again at the mercy of strangers.

FIVE

I wake slowly, realizing the rain has stopped, bombarded with thoughts, both old and new. Last night is the first real night of sleep I've had since the night before I fought Soren. So much has happened. The Fall Gauntlet feels like a far-off dream.

Musty sunlight streams through the windows. I get up to see what kind of damage the rain has done, but there's no flooding of any kind. The ground is darker, soggier, but other than that, it's like last night's murderous downpour never happened. My thoughts are with Soren, so I go to him immediately, but when I open the door, I'm surprised to see Miki.

She wears a loose-fitting tunic with long sleeves, a good lightweight choice for the heat, and I've been given something similar. A single pin holds her hair in place atop her head but some strands are loose, giving her bangs. She smiles at me. "Benji," she says.

She's as beautiful as she is confident. I can't place my feelings right now, which is rare. Am I intimidated?

Jealous? Nervous because I've never been around such a pretty girl like her?

"I wanted to apologize for my outburst earlier," Miki says. "May I come in?"

What has she seen in her eighteen years that I haven't?

"It's your spa," I say before catching myself. "I mean, of course. You can do whatever you want."

Miki enters and stops in front of me. Her eyes swirl with a sadness I cannot place, one that is different from Lyaza's sadness. But with Miki, there is something else too. Anger? Rage?

"I can be passionate about the Dei, and sometimes I lose my cool. I suppose I'm frustrated because of what happened in the capital while I'm here, unable to do anything about it."

"Really, it's okay. Passion is good." I say, rolling my wrists in circles to get the blood flowing.

"You traveled from New Phasia," Miki says, her voice urgent. "What was happening? Did you notice any kind of interference from the gods and goddesses?" Her eyes plead with me, hungry for new information.

I need to be very careful.

For one, I don't want to say the wrong thing about the Dei, or mistakenly insult them and anger Miki. And two, if Miki identifies us as the brothers who wrecked the entire Fall Gauntlet, things will not end well. It will end with Soren and me on the streets, or our throats slit in our sleep. As much as I hate to admit it, we need these girls' help.

"I didn't notice anything," I say, holding Miki's gaze. "But we were trying to get out as fast as possible. The city was chaotic. People were rioting, looting—I don't think people knew what to do." I think about the flurry of events that led to Soren and me ending up in the sewers, meeting the rats, Dr. Fitz, and the old lady with the violin, and learning about the so-called manufactured champions that will come to hunt my brother and me for what we've done—all of it seems so unbelievable. I feel the urge to tell Miki some of it but hold back. A more pressing question comes to my mind. "What's going to happen now? I mean, with the Dei and everything? Do you really think they'll show themselves?"

"I do," Miki says, her hands clasped in front of her. "They're already starting to. Can you hear the thunder in the distance?" Miki turns to the window at the far end of the room as bold rays of sunlight burn over the mountains.

"Yes," I say. As if on cue, rain pelts the small square of window.

"This is how it begins," Miki says. "First, the tears of the holy cleanse the world of sin. Then, their wrath comes down to Calypso as fire and lightning."

"But can't it just be weather? How do you know it's them?" I feel these are natural questions.

Miki's gaze snaps back to me, and it's so intense I think she may decide to snap my neck. When she speaks it's not with anger, though. "I can feel it, Benji," she says with a wry smile, as though she is their chosen vessel for their messages of lightning and thunder. "Haven't you ever been able to feel something so deep in your bones—and you don't need any fact or human to validate or confirm what you feel—you just know it to be true?"

Like Mom still being alive.

I nod, unable to speak for the present moment.

"Then you know what I'm talking about. Without a champion, the Harvest cycle won't change. When the Harvest cycle doesn't change, the seasons fall out of balance."

"But why? If it's never happened before, how do you know what will happen? Maybe the Dei will just keep doing what they're doing and not notice." I want to save my mom and am prepared to take down more champions to get her, but I didn't factor any gods or goddesses into the equation.

"Things that don't normally happen are happening," Miki says. "Haven't you noticed that?"

It's a vague sentiment but a memory strikes me then, the moment when I generated electricity with my gem staff. That had never happened in the gauntlet. The voice I heard yesterday is new too.

CRACK

Outside, a streak of lightning rips through the air, and thunder makes me jump. The sky is wondrously blue and bright for a brief moment, and then the drizzle intensifies into a downpour. Rain strikes the roof in rapid bursts. The sound is calming.

Miki places a hand on her sternum, her mouth agape as she looks out the window.

"How do we stop it?" I ask, needing to know now. I need Miki's knowledge while we're still here.

"We have to honor them," Miki says, turning to face me again. She clasps her hands together as if in prayer, steepling her fingers. "Do you know how the Fall Gauntlet usually just features the same champions over and over," Miki begins. "That's because the Crown has always tried their best to honor the Dei with the relics they have."

"Relics?"

"The masks, Benji."

I hold Miki's gaze. "With the ones they have? Are you saying that—"

"There are more relics out there."

Thunder booms and lightning lights up the gray sky as rain falls with a vengeance.

"What do the Dei care about more relics? They can have whatever they want if what we're taught about them is true."

"They don't want the relics," Miki says. "They want to be honored. They live their own divine lives away from us. The Fall Gauntlet is their way of watching us, and we make sacrifices. They know we'll continue to make prayers in their name, and we know they'll keep us safe from some of the more devious deities."

Miki knows things. Mom used to talk about the different deities, and now it's coming back to me. The Harvest cycle allows the Dei to keep order within their own realm. I still have questions, questions I would ask my Mom if she were still here.

"But we're just one world."

"And there are guardians of this world," Miki says. "When we don't keep order, it may look to them like we don't care about them or want to rise up against them."

Maybe we should.

I feel anger rise inside of me for what they've done to Mom. To Dad. I need to tell Soren.

The cycle of killing each other for sport just so the gods and goddesses can feel their power over us seems barbaric. And yet, it's a tradition I always wanted to partake in. I never cared about what it really was. All I cared about was winning and saving Mom. Maybe Miki is right that the gauntlet should be broken.

"What about the wish part?" I ask, still needing Miki's knowledge while it's accessible. "How does that work?"

Miki shakes her head. "I must admit I don't know. *The Book of Totems* speaks of wishes granted, so I know it's part of the bargain. I just don't know how it plays out."

That's because the winners become the Crown's slaves, I think. I recall my last conversation with D, and my chest suddenly aches. My days down in the tunnels seem so much simpler.

Miki smiles, her eyes sharp with intrigue. "Benji, there's a legend that speaks of one of the Originals making sacrifice around these parts. In the mountains on the way out of town. I can feel its spirit. If I can contact its spirit, I may be able to contact the Dei too."

It takes me a moment to understand what Miki is telling me.

I haven't thought about the Originals, the first of the animals that walked Calypso, the ones from which all lesser animals evolved, in a long time. There was a time I was obsessed with them and memorized their pages in books, the lore and legends surrounding each one. "You're saying the Originals' spirit is going to help you commune with the Dei? How do you figure that?"

"The Originals are the bridge between the Dei and us," Miki says. "Their spiritual energy could be enough to make contact."

"But they're gone. The Originals went to other worlds. What do you mean by 'making a sacrifice?'" It's hard not to think that both the Dei and the Originals have abandoned our world.

Miki shakes her head. "Sometimes they can come back. Some have passed beyond the veil for good, and all that remains are their descendants, the greater and lesser animals. But some have just hidden themselves from us."

Is that why the condor's ceremony is here in Oajin?

My head is spinning. I've never read about any of this in *The Book of Totems.* I wonder where Miki's gotten her information. I humor her. "Okay, let's say you can commune or connect or whatever with this Original, and the Dei somehow show themselves to the"—I search for the words Miki used earlier—"likes of us peasants. Then what?"

Miki's expression is cold and determined as she fixes her eyes on mine. "Then I can humbly ask what sort of penance they seek."

She has no idea how mad she sounds.

Her plan seems pointless. Why ask the Dei how we can serve them, if they're already going to be angry at us— mainly me—for breaking the Fall Gauntlet tournament and ending the Harvest cycle?

Miki tells me about chores she needs help with for the day and when breakfast will be ready, then leaves me alone. I barely hear her. My mind is somewhere else, digesting all of this new information.

Soren and I have a plan to get to the Tangerine Islands to stop a powerful nanotech maker, who's apparently manufacturing new masks by the day, but what if the Dei arrive before that? I wonder if Miki is right, if somehow we need to get ahead of this growing problem and appeal to the Dei, or at least show them what's in our hearts before it's too late. If the lynx mask hadn't chosen me in the temple, I probably never would have believed in something like that.

If the Dei really are out there and want us to fall in line, what choice do I have? Go back to the capital and surrender? Let the Crown force Soren or me into becoming the one true champion? It seems too late for all that. I need answers, and I know where to find them. Where I always find them.

With the lynx.

I dig through my things in the makeshift satchel holding the rat mask and the camo sleeves Lyaza gave me and fish out my own mask. The ancient piece of technology is like lead in my hand, heavy and unforgiving. I press it to my face without hesitation. The integration process jolts my body, and I feel like I am being sucked into a different universe, like the mask is a vacuum in space and I am falling into it. My body is sore, exhausted, and underfed, but so hungry for the mask's power, and the process is more painful than usual as my neurons fray and pierce my temples. My bones ring and my teeth gnash as I bite back pain.

Then it's over.

I exhale in a huff and take in my new surroundings. If things that don't normally happen are happening now, the lynx will be able to see those things. I hope. My aura field pulses in near silence as I rotate around the room, looking for clues, some disturbance that will make my mask react. The outside world is a kaleidoscope of orange circles vibrating out in even patterns. I have not seen much orange within my aura field and have never seen concentric circles—usually there are blue lines elongating then collapsing as they show me probabilities of what is to come.

The circles pulsate outward.

Time moves slower.

The oranges darken.

Red blooms like thousands of roses opening, a sudden gushing of red wine. Rivers flood banks. *What am I seeing?*

The rivers turn red. Bloody. A dense shape passes overhead, the blood-red moon, darkening, sucking in all light.

Come to me. Please, come to me.

That voice again. Closer than before. In my ear. In my head.

The others have kept me here.

I see things, quick glimpses, half-images. Fire scorches homes, burning them down. Ash and smoke fill the sky. I can't see it, but I feel a rush of energy as something approaches me, some entity, raw with power.

I'm bound to this place.

Jaws open wide.

Fiery irises smolder in the endless pit of night.

Release me from these shackles.

I have to leave this place. My aura field is gone. It feels like I'm falling into outer space, unable to breathe. I scream inside this dark new world, but outside I'm in an invisible straitjacket, unable to move or make a sound.

The world grows dark.

My breath is caught.

I hit the ground, reeling in pain as I writhe on the floor, clutching my throat. My mask clatters to the ground. I cough for what seems like forever. The lynx mask lies dormant, staring at me from the floor. Did I take it off? I have no memory of it.

That was not at all what I expected to happen.

Something is not right about this place. The rain has stopped. Am I hallucinating?

I catch my breath, get my bearings, and get dressed for the day in lightweight pants and a shirt that have been laid out for me. I pay Soren a quick visit before one of the sisters can tell me not to. Or put me to work. He's still sleeping. I shake him awake. Opening his eyes slowly, he looks at me like he has no idea who I am.

"Soren, get up. We have to talk."

My bear of a brother exhales a night's worth of air out his nostrils then says, "That was the craziest dream I've had in my entire life."

Seems like we have a lot to talk about.

SIX

I tell Soren everything: about the voice I heard when we first arrived in Oajin, how Miki plans to commune with the Dei, and finally, how we're by and large enemy number one. And two.

Soren already knows the last one. The voice and communing with the Dei are more puzzling to him. He's sitting on his bed, chin resting in his hands as he gazes ahead with a blank stare. "So you think the voice came from the Dei? That's interesting. My dream was kinda about the same thing."

I'm leaning against the wall, staring out the window while keeping an eye on Soren in front of me. The sun continues to climb over the mountain as the gray sky brightens to a pale azure. "What was your dream?"

Soren shakes his head, which is still cradled in his hands. "It felt so real. This lady was there. Taking care of me. I was hurt, lying on the ground. There was a big forest clearing, a bright moon. She looked down at me, and it felt so real. Her eyes—they were so big, so kind." Soren rises to his feet. "I was dying, bro." He says it as though he's just realizing it.

"Who was she? Someone you've met or seen before?" I ask. "Most people we see in dreams are people we already know."

"I didn't know her," Soren says, his eyes wide and battling the thoughts in his head. "Or at least I don't think I did. She said she needed help, needed to be set free." Soren looks up, a sudden realization washing over him. "I think she was a goddess or something, Benji."

That's when something clicks in my own brain. "The Fallen Goddess," I say.

"Yeah," Soren says, barely above a whisper. The dream has clearly touched him in some way. He's slower, more pensive and careful. "How did you know that? That's who she was. I could feel that from her. She fell from the heavens and couldn't get back."

"Sounds rough," I say. "I know about the Fallen Goddess because Lyaza mentioned her yesterday. I think it's time to learn a little more."

Downstairs, we eat a breakfast of fried rice with eggs and pickled cabbage. Soren and I are starved, so it's hard for us to speak with our mouths full. Before we even have a chance to ask about the Fallen Goddess, Miki tells us our chores for the day. Our duties include chopping wood and building part of a shed that they're going to use for growing plants.

"You're still sick and need to rest," Miki says to Soren.

When I look at him, I know she's right. Soren doesn't argue. His face blanches and he runs to the bathroom. I turn to Lyaza, who's been quiet all morning. "Are you okay?"

"I'm fine," Lyaza says, not meeting my gaze. "I'm going into town today to buy some food and other things we need for the spa." She excuses herself from the table, grabs her backpack and leaves without another word.

I'm alone with Miki. "Let's start with the shed. I want to have part of it covered so I can start planting in there."

We work all day. It's not the most grueling work, just a lot of hammering, nailing, measuring, and assisting Miki as she builds a shed behind the spa. It's not much different from building contraptions around the shop with Master Gherus. I miss him and D. I miss a simpler time, being around people who truly want to help me. I'm not sure what Miki wants other than to speak with the Dei and repent.

Around sundown, I chop as much wood as I can. The exercise is good for me and my body welcomes the challenge. It's not until after dinner that I'm able to finally get Lyaza alone and ask her about the Fallen Goddess.

She's sitting on the steps outside, watching the sun sink behind the mountains. Part of me feels like she's been waiting for me. I don't wait to say what I need, not when Miki is inside clearing the table and could come out at any moment. Taking a seat next to Lyaza, I ask, "You mentioned the Fallen Goddess the other day and said you'd tell me more. Who is she?"

Lyaza's breaths are shallow, as though she's been crying, or will start crying any second. Something seems off about her as she hugs her knees to her chest, chin resting on top. While Miki is beautiful and striking, Lyaza is pretty and plain. Her jet-black hair cut to her shoulders frames her round face and the smattering of freckles on her cheeks.

"The Fallen Goddess used to be a goddess, but she fell," Lyaza begins. "She fell from grace or the heavens or something—no one knows—but she ..." Lyaza hesitates, looking at me for the first time. "She stopped being a goddess. Is how the legend goes anyway."

167

"Okay, so … Miki wants to find her, commune with her, ask her what the rest of the Dei are up to?"

Lyaza forces a laugh. "You really don't know my sister. Miki doesn't want to commune with the Fallen Goddess. She wants to *become* the new goddess."

Now it's my turn to laugh. "How does someone become a goddess? That's absurd." Mom used to tell us stories about the Dei: the wrathful ones, the merciful ones. Could some of them have been conflicted?

"If that's what you think, then this conversation is over," Lyaza says. Her sadness is gone and her sass is back.

"Okay, sorry. I'm just a little new to this," I say. "Can Miki really do that?"

"With the Fallen Goddess gone, a spot has opened up." Lyaza says this like it's the most obvious thing in the world. "Miki will stop at nothing to get what she wants. I know this."

We're quiet for a moment. The breeze rustles our hair.

"What happened to your parents?" I ask.

At first, Lyaza says nothing. I think she may not answer me, but then she turns, her face downcast as she wrings her hands.

"The Crown took them away from us," Lyaza says, her voice devoid of emotion. Lyaza is difficult to read. I thought that when I met her on the train, and I think it again now.

I wait to see if she will say more. She doesn't. "That's something we have in common."

My admission is enough for Lyaza to keep going.

"It happened four years ago when we lived in the capital. I was nine and Miki was thirteen. Our parents were servants in the outer circle but their skills were nothing out of the ordinary. It just happened one night." Lyaza sighs, like reliving the memory is too painful but she continues on. "Miki had bad feelings about what was happening. Our parents had been coming home later and later, whispering secrets in the dark. Then one day they were just gone. They didn't come back. No one told Miki or me anything."

"They can't just do that," I say, my old and rageful sentiments about how horrible the Crown is and how we need to take them down resurfacing.

"The Crown takes what they want. Miki tried to find out what happened. She tried to get our parents back." Lyaza squeezes her hands together, as though in pain. Like there is something she's still not telling me.

"So your parents may still be alive." It's not a question.

"Benji, listen to me," Lyaza says, not answering me directly. "Miki thinks that she can commune with the Dei and replace the Fallen Goddess."

"Do *you* think she can?" I ask.

"I think that she's going to get herself killed," Lyaza says, and now finally, I can place the sadness she holds tonight. She both loves and fears Miki. She fears losing her. "She's crazy enough to try and get hit by lightning, because she thinks that will bring her closer to them. Or she'll burn herself in the hot springs. Miki is surprising enough to try anything at this point."

"What else is there to try?" I ask.

Rain sprinkles down.

We both stand. She looks at the graying sky, then fixes her eyes on me. "She'll hunt those brothers from the Fall Gauntlet tournament. She'll kill them. Everyone is saying that defeating them means there will be a champion. And their wish will be granted."

Lyaza knows this about her sister and yet Miki said nothing about that as an option. She was hiding parts of her hand.

Miki knows who we are.

"Benji, are you okay?" Lyaza asks, trying to get a look at me.

I don't answer. I'm already running inside, shaking off the rainwater, bounding up the steps, and bursting into Soren's room. Soren is asleep again, but I don't care. There's enough light outside for us to run to the train station and get out of this city. We need to get away from Miki. After our run-in with the rat, I'm not risking our lives again.

"Soren, wake up."

Soren stirs, coughing on his own drool, then rolls over and mumbles something incomprehensible.

"We have to leave. Get up."

Soren doesn't move this time. I'm surprised to see Lyaza enter the room, alarm on her face as she rushes over to me.

"I don't think it's a good idea to move him, Benji," Lyaza says, grabbing my wrists.

I shake her off of me, my anger rearing its ugly head. "What's wrong with him? Why can't anyone tell me what's wrong with him!"

"Because we don't know," Lyaza says. "Tell me what happened to him and let me help."

My emotions are a storm raging inside me. I don't want to trust anyone. Not Lyaza, not Miki, not Daniil. Just Soren. I want to leave with Soren. We're not strangers to stealing or finding food.

I say nothing. I'm not explaining the masks to Lyaza. I have no idea where her loyalties lie. If she knows we're the bear and the lynx, she may very well side with Miki and try to end us.

It doesn't matter. Soren is out cold. Outside, another downpour graces the night with its presence. I'm in my room the next moment, raging and confused, afraid that my decision will lead us to more trouble or, worse, to Soren dying.

I can't take it. This feels too big, too heavy for me to solve on my own. When did everything become so complicated? It's been a long day, so I try to calm my emotions so that they don't override my rational thoughts.

I go about the rest of the night as if nothing has happened, even though Lyaza knows something has. If I'm going to get us out of here, I need to be more careful about not giving us away, so I become the good little boy the Crown always wanted me to be. I bathe, washing the filth off my body, then I eat, devouring pork and rice at dinner. Lyaza and Miki talk to each other and leave me alone.

I finish eating in record time, my thoughts a mangled mess, then bring Soren his food. I try my best to shake him awake so he can eat, but he's out cold. I want to stay with him, but it hurts to see him like this, and besides, I need more answers.

Retiring to my room, I put on my mask. Quiet overtakes my brain space as mask integration takes place, and then I hear the voice, soft and pleading.

Come to me. Come to the mountains on the full moon, and the goddess will appear to a worthy champion.

The full moon is tomorrow. I conserve my energy until then, and Miki pauses the outdoor chores due to the ongoing rain, so I spend my time visiting my sleeping brother and getting rest myself. My body is tired and begs for sleep, but my mind is on edge, playing out all possible scenarios and outcomes, as though I am in the gauntlet again.

On the day of the full moon, I prepare to go to the mountains to see if the goddess will appear to me. I am a champion of sorts, even though neither Soren nor I technically won. If I can speak with the goddess directly, and she decides that I am worthy, maybe I don't need the Crown to grant my wish.

After dinner, I go to my room and put on my mask, only to find that Miki is about to make her move. She emerges from her room downstairs wearing a skin-tight jumpsuit as black as night, with only her eyes exposed. A whip hangs from a holster at her waist.

The rain outside hammers the roof, the walls, but it doesn't stop Miki. The next moment she's gone. I thought she might head to the mountains soon since she mentioned it, so I'm already prepared to go, my battle tunic and clothes now washed. I grab my gauntlets and gem staff. Then I'm outside in the pouring rain, which seems like nothing compared to my nervous excitement, while a goddess talks to me, calling me to her.

I put on my mask.

The transition is nothing. I become the lynx in seconds, ignoring any pain or pull on my human form. Rain soaks me to the bone.

Please, you must come quickly.

I need to make contact, not Miki. Should I have considered her more of a threat?

I run. Vector lines surge forward in the direction of the mountains. Nothing else. Chi Spa is closer to the edge of Oajin so it doesn't take me long, maybe ten minutes, to run to the edge of town. There is a dirt trail leading to the mountains, which are a few miles away. The ground is sturdier than the sand dunes that surround Oajin. Water sloshes at my feet. Mud threatens to pull my boots deeper into the ground. Perhaps Miki is as lost as Lyaza thinks she is. I don't know what I can do to bring her back, but maybe I can stop her from becoming a goddess.

I never thought I'd have that thought in this lifetime.

My aura field sputters then. The light blue flashes and goes dark, then the world blinks black. It's like all probabilities become zero. Or everything is possible. A light flashes above my head and streaks across the horizon like lightning, which is impossible. Lightning doesn't move that way. The light flashes again, and I realize that it's not lightning. I've seen that light before.

A hoverboard. Zooming toward the mountains.

I don't think it's a coincidence.

I'm not stupid enough to think that the voice is only talking to me.

SEVEN

When I reach the mountains half an hour later, my boots are heavy, caked in mud and dirt, and my soaked clothes weigh me down, but I don't stop. The sky is dark except for the moon, whose bulbous white light illuminates the massive blur of mountains looming ahead. Under the hazy sheen of rain, the mountain's silhouette is a darkened series of flat valleys and jagged peaks.

Numbers whirl through my aura field, informing me of distances and probabilities, as they always do, but I take more notice now. The mountains reach an elevation of about 8,000 feet with moderate elevation gain. They look small from where I stand, but falling from them will certainly be fatal.

Catching my breath, I survey my surroundings. Hot pools dot the mountain's base, and I know there are more I can't see. Amidst pounding rain and turbulent lightning, I spot the neon lights I saw earlier, floating cautiously and ascending the mountain. I don't see Miki, but I'm dying to know what brought Daniil here.

Ignoring the lightning and my mounting fear, I climb slick rocks, scaling the mountain with the help of my gauntlets, gripping and pulling myself up to a flat area interspersed with hot springs that hiss and steam under the blanket of rainfall. I don't want to find out how hot they are. The soft hum of the hoverboard has died. I want to call for Daniil but think better of it. I wish he weren't here. I don't want him involved in this.

A silhouette emerges, scrambling over the other side to join me at this level, stark against the mountainous backdrop.

Miki. Has she been waiting for me?

I don't have Soren here this time to help me. I have to stop Miki from becoming a goddess.

Miki steps forward, her clothing slick and gleaming like leather, a skintight hood wrapped around her head. She holds a whip that is coiled around her hand, the end hanging down like the tongue of a lizard.

"So, the lynx has graced us here in Oajin with his presence," Miki says.

She's not a big girl. She's older than me by a year but is a few inches shorter and much smaller. Not petite, but not exactly muscular either. I realize I don't know her at all.

"Miki," I say, my voice slightly modified by my mask's tech. "You don't have to do this. You don't know what it will take to become a goddess. You don't know what you could lose."

Even as I say it, I struggle to wrap my mind around how a human even becomes a deity.

"I know what's on the other side of doing nothing," she says, and I hear the venom growing in her voice. She looks to the sky, her face glowing like its own small moon, her hands clasped in prayer, and says, "Oh holy ones, hear my prayer. Make me your worthy servant. I shall honor you and serve you all my days. Sacrifice!" It sounds like an incantation. Miki clasps her hands over her chest, then lowers her head and chin in silent reverence.

Lightning strikes and crackles in the distance. Thunder rumbles past the mountains. A single hot spring thirty feet long stands between Miki and me.

When Miki's prayer is over, her eyes flick up. Then she crouches low and sprints at me, bounding across rocks, her whip out and trailing behind her like a reptilian tail until she is upon me.

My aura field shows me probabilities, but there are blues and oranges and yellows now, a combination of circles and lines and vortices, collapsing into each other as one whirling image. I try to parse out the details but there isn't time.

She snaps her wrist, and her whip unfurls from her hand like a lashing tongue, so much longer than I imagined, as it swirls above me like a boa waiting to strike.

SNAP! She whips my back.

All I can do is gasp for air as I reel in pain. She yanks my gem staff from my hand with a quick snap of her whip and hurls it behind her with incredible force. The staff spins in the air like its nothing, not an ancient weapon passed down from the gods, but a pencil, spiraling up and disappearing into the blackness of night.

My aura field is a mess of colors competing for the stage, and I can't make sense of any of it.

Above us, rocks rumble and shift from their beds, grinding against each other. My stomach is knotted with anxiety and confusion as I attempt to locate my staff while tracking the rumbling sound and worrying about rocks falling on my head. Did lightning split a rock in two? I don't have to wait long to get my answer.

A beam of light surges and shoots skyward above us, blasting toward the heavens. I have never seen anything like it.

Yes, that's it. You found me, faithful servant. You finally found me.

The voice is back, but there's mischief in it this time, not the sweet, caring lilt of a goddess. Why does everything tonight feel like a bad omen?

I wonder if Miki can hear it too, but she's gone, leaping and swinging her whip like a grappling apparatus as she scales the mountain higher. She's a whirling jet-black image, a cross between a black widow spider and a viper snake.

My muscles fire and I become the lynx, springing into action, following her up the mountain in feline ways, jumping like a cat, gripping wet stone, pulling myself up high, and launching myself to the next landing, sensing the presence of my staff as I do. When I arrive where I saw the light, Miki is already there, back turned, and is staring at something on the ground. Beyond her, neon yellow lights blink on and off, giving shape to another familiar figure floating in midair.

Daniil.

Oh no.

By some mechanism I don't understand, I see what Miki is holding without seeing it with my eyes, as though I'm seeing through her. Now I finally realize what Daniil is after. What they are both after.

A mask.

My aura field snaps into probability precognition and bursts like a red balloon, propelling red shrapnel spikes across Miki's body, as my body tingles with knowledge it hasn't yet told me.

"No, Miki! Don't!"

Daniil leans forward and rushes Miki, but she's too quick, snapping her whip at Daniil like he is a fly to be crushed. The whip nails him in the chest and, as if time is slowed, I hear wind leave his body, the sickening crack of bone. He goes sailing off his hoverboard and over the edge.

"You can't just—" I lose my breath. *Daniil.*

Miki holds the mask out in front of her, mesmerized. The twinkle in her eyes is gone, replaced with something more sinister. The mask is in her hands, and then not—it's on her face as she inhales sharply. I can finally see the totem animal now. I remember the reptilian statues outside of the spa.

Chrysix.

Ancient creatures said to hold fire in their bellies for heating pools and burning off toxins. Now it all makes sense. Miki moans and claws at the mask on her face.

My mind is connecting dots at a furious pace as I consider what it means that there's a totem mask outside the Fall Gauntlet. The Crown doesn't know about it. Has someone been hiding it?

Miki's body lurches forward and her limbs flail. The voice from before laughs, breaking the dense silence inside my mask.

This body will do.

The voice is the same as before, but more unhinged and wilder, and that's when I realize that the Fallen Goddess was never calling us. The chrysix mask was.

"Stop! She doesn't want you. She wanted the goddess, not you," I say, words spilling out of me as my eyesight sharpens, as I feel myself become more beast than human.

The masks have their own spirit. Each one is codified to one champion at a time. You're either chosen or you're not, but I've never seen the struggle go on this long. The integration of mask and human combines psychohistory and genetics, and the first time is always the most painful.

"What are you? You're not a totem animal," I say. I want the integration to fail so I can bring Miki back to Lyaza. I don't want her to become the chrysix.

Miki stops convulsing, straightens her back, and stands tall.

This time, when I hear the voice, it isn't in my head. This time it comes from the mask itself, from Miki.

"You think you're so clever, little lynx, but you know nothing," Miki says, snarling. "And you followed like the good little lifesaver you are. You wouldn't believe how hard it is to get another totem mask up here."

Miki snorts and exhales sharply, like she's fighting herself.

She clutches the sides of her face as though she'll rip the mask off and discard this new reptilian version of herself.

I have never seen a totem mask outside of the temples where people must speak their sacrifice to the gods and goddesses so that the mask will choose them. And yet, Miki spoke her sacrifice out here in the wild.

I want to leave and find Daniil, but something keeps me there.

I want to know what this means. I need to learn about the hidden layers of the Fall Gauntlet.

"GRANT ME THINE POWER, OH HOLY ONES!" Miki screams skyward, her entire body heaving.

The night grows quiet. Miki looks up and cocks her head to one side. Her breathing slows. She no longer holds the mask or tries to remove it. My aura field shows convergence, two orbiting bodies colliding in a cosmic blue flash of light. Her prayer worked.

The chrysix chose her.

"Miki, you don't have to do this," I say, unsure who I'm even talking to now. If I bring Miki back to Lyaza as her sister asked, I will need to defeat her. I won't kill her, just knock her out, remove her mask and get her home. It worked with Soren in the gauntlet, why can't it work here?

"Oh but I do, little lynx," Miki says. Her voice is loud above the rain and distant thunder. "I have waited for this moment for so long, and now—" She looks down at her hands, which sport no gauntlets. All she has is her whip, which she brought herself—not the ancient weapon coupled with the chrysix mask. "Now, I'm back."

The chrysix mask shares the same terrifying features of a monitor lizard with its powerful jaws and forked tongue. I remember seeing it in *The Book of Totems*, a fiery creature born from dragons and komodos, a more evolved version that grew smaller and hid from the aggressive tendencies of humans in order to survive while still retaining its lethal nature. I don't know its incantations or its weaknesses, but I have an idea of what they might be.

Miki laughs a hoarse laugh. "And it's all because of you. Benji." Her voice is deadlier, filled with the dread of endless night.

I need my gem staff to defeat her, and see that it's landed behind her, nestled between two rocks above us. I attempt to stall. "What are you talking about?"

"I knew if I, or rather, if Miki, challenged you directly you might not come. But if I lured both of you here by making you think the Fallen Goddess was calling, I knew it was only a matter of time."

"To what end? What's the point of luring me here?"

"To break me free from my shackles," Miki—the chrysix—says, pointing to her mask. "You don't know what happened, do you? You don't have any idea how these things work, do you?" Miki laughs wickedly, and I'm afraid for what she is becoming.

I step forward, my hand raised. My aura field is expanding beyond the mountain's pointed edges and plateaus, and I'm receiving information about my surroundings, about future probabilities I will need to decide on. "I know that the Fall Gauntlet is over, the Harvest is over, and the Dei have abandoned us." I need to anger Miki now. I need her to resurface. I need to insult the Dei so she will wake up and fight back. Even if it means fighting me.

"The Dei *have* abandoned scum of the soil like you!" She spits her insult. "The totems," she says again, pointing. "They want to find each other. When they do, they lock themselves in battle. This is the *real* way of the gauntlet."

The rain falls. I let her words sink in.

"There can be only one victor," she says. "Winning means freedom."

So that's it. The mask, lost to humankind for centuries, buried underneath these mountains—perhaps from a previous gauntlet battle—would finally show itself when a worthy opponent entered the fray. *Me.*

"If this is the way of the gauntlet, then let it happen as it should," I say, a spark of rage burning inside me. "As usual, the Dei are not here. The rain and lightning are not them." I look skyward. "Show yourselves. You don't give a damn about us down here. You let us kill each other senselessly by pulling the Crown's strings like they're puppets. But we're the ones doing the fighting, not you!"

Angering the Miki-chrysix works better than I could have hoped.

She lunges at me, her voice a rattling shriek. "You shut your dirty peasant mouth!"

That's a new one.

I think my mask will show me her movements, the trajectory, but she's faster than anything I've seen. A blur of black against an even darker sky. I feel pain in my torso where she slashes me and draws blood. She may not have gauntlets but the girl's got nails.

"Oh holy ones, know my heart and raise me up," Miki says. "I only win with you." She's behind me now. I took her attack so that I could make a run for my staff. Let her make her prayers to the holy ones. I sprint as fast as I can, bounding up makeshift staircases of slippery rock—

SNAP!

I go down hard.

Her whip has ripped through my shirt and torn open my skin. I do everything I can to bite back the pain that seems endless, pushing myself up off my stomach and gasping for air. My aura field erupts with new colors and shapes as I stand, clutch my side and turn to face Miki.

"When I kill you," Miki says, her chest heaving. "I will be the new Fall Gauntlet champion, and the Harvest cycle will begin anew. One where fire purges the land, and the chrysix reigns over peasants like you!" Miki is gone, her voice now deep like the mines and tunnels underneath us.

I sprint for my staff.

Miki's whip is up and out, slashing toward me as my aura field collapses inward like a black hole. There is one way to dodge. Throwing my weight forward, I step hard and flip sideways into an aerial, narrowly missing the whip's strike, and landing with only a split second to close the distance between me and the staff before Miki strikes again.

I lunge for my staff, snatching it, then turning to face the attack, my body pure momentum and motion. My aura field narrows, blue vector lines crash like waves, and I grip tightly, knowing the force will be enough to knock me off this mountain. Just like Daniil...

The whip hits my staff, sending a shock reverberating through my bones and ears. The world erupts with the noise of rain, the thunder, the crack of whip pounding in my skull, then plunges into silence and everything is muted, like I am underwater, until my ears finally stop ringing. I know that Miki intends to kill me. Can I actually bring her back to Lyaza or is it too late for that? What will Lyaza do when she finds out I killed her sister? What would I do?

"Miki, please. If you want to commune with the Dei, do you really think this is the way?"

"This is their plan. I have become one with the chrysix so that I may carry out their will!" Miki begins convulsing, and her mask glows a smoldering cherry, like there is magma underneath. She clutches at her throat like she's about to choke on a stone, her neck bulging, then she stops.

She's completely still as she stares me down.

One of the blue lines in my aura field spikes low and long, showing me that her next attack will have a small probability of hitting me, but there's something about how the line stays spiked that makes me sprint for cover behind a rock. She rears back like she's about to spit on me, and then—

Fire.

The dark night explodes into a mosaic of brilliant red and orange light as she unleashes fire as volatile as a volcanic eruption from her mouth. I drop to the ground and slide underneath the ball of fire that singes my body before I careen across the slick rocks to cover.

My heart is pounding, and I'm afraid for what I'm about to do. What if the Dei really are angry, and they want to end me now? If that's the truth, then what else can I do but end this fight before it ends me?

When I step out from cover, I notice Miki's launched herself onto a rocky perch above us, down on all fours, but it's clear that Miki is gone. And she's changing again right before my eyes.

A tail begins to grow out of her.

Any thought that Miki is not the chosen one is squashed.

She's becoming the chrysix.

Her tail grows longer, fattening like a snake that's just swallowed its prey. She doesn't seem fazed at all. Her hands cling to the rock, her tail waving in the air as she shoots her next fireball.

All I can do to save myself from being blasted off this mountain is hold out my gem staff, my one final protection. When the fireball hits the staff's rod, it ricochets off, but the force blows me back. I slide across the slick rocks to the edge, slamming my rod into the ground to slow me down.

The next fireball comes.

It's as if time slows. My aura field is calm. Annoyingly calm. I don't have time to think about my options. I swing my gem staff at the incoming fireball, but mistime it, my vision a blur, and clip the front end of the fiery orb, trying to squash it. What happens next is strange. The part of the fireball that I hit with my staff speeds back at Miki, who doesn't expect it, but she's still fast enough to crawl down the rock to avoid it. The other part of the fireball gets absorbed when it hits the gem cradled at the top of the staff's rod, causing it to glow, like an aquamarine brain pulsing with electrical energy, now activated. I know the staff can generate exponential force, but can it absorb other energy sources?

If it can, it's new to me.

"Can't you see that the Dei want me to win?" Miki says, snarling. "I am their chosen champion. When I destroy you like the weak human you are, I'll be free to roam as before."

My breath is a knot in my chest. I'm sucking in as much oxygen as I can, wondering if she's right. Fear roils through my body like a heatwave. I've never been this afraid to die because I never thought I'd lose in the gauntlet. I couldn't afford to. With Miki, I'm afraid. I'm afraid that she—the chrysix—is right about the Dei and they'll strike me down. I thought I knew the gauntlet, but this brings an entirely new element to the battles. I have never grown any kind of tail. Only the mask's holoskin has given me pointed ears and a furry face.

Miki stands and cracks her whip at me. I intuit the attack and sidestep. Her tail comes next, like a monstrous cobra coming down from the sky. Sidestepping again, the tail lands with a thud beside me, spraying debris and sloshing water, then swinging back to Miki in a long, powerful arc above me.

"Holy mammals," I say. The force of it is enough to shatter my skull.

Miki plans to blast me off this mountain. Her whip, which she's now spit some kind of oily liquid ooze on, bursts into orange and red flame as she lights it on fire with a quick breath. The rain sputters to a sprinkle, as if I need any more signs that the Dei are against me.

I don't know how I'm supposed to win this. I don't know if I'm supposed to win.

Miki is evolving and learning abilities and mutating at an insane velocity. I, on the other hand, am still learning how to use my staff and become more like the lynx. Once again, I see where my training has been inadequate, how this twisted new version of the Fall Gauntlet is much more wildly unpredictable.

Miki's vine of a tail, her vicious fast whip, and the fireballs she spits from her mouth that burst and blaze with heat and beautiful fiery colors all create chaos in my aura field. She comes at me with every attack imaginable. Her tail and whip bite at my body like giant killer wasps, ripping skin away every time they make contact. The fireballs torpedo toward me, threatening to send me to a watery grave below as I swing my staff and send them back at her harder and faster.

SNAP!

She thwacks my thigh with her whip, tearing my shorts and skin underneath. Then she spits her fireballs. I dodge the first, the second, then send the third one back. She smacks it back at me with her tail, and I take cover behind a rock. My vision is a whirling blur and my aura field pulses oblong blues, the vector lines rearranging into new shapes, trying to show me something. My aura field, my connection with the lynx is how I made it to the finals of the Fall Gauntlet. It is how I escaped.

It is how I win now.

Through fire and darkness and lacerations, the holy trinity of my new pain, time slows. I step out from my rock cover, and see my aura field calm, slowly unraveling, opening up to a single but obscure probability. I don't know what Miki will do next, but I know I need to meet it with my gem staff.

"See how the Dei love me?" Miki says as she slithers toward me. "See how they want me to end you—the lynx—the standing champion of the Fall Gauntlet? See how they've forsaken you?" We have battled our way to a narrow and deadly landing. Twenty feet between us. Two paces to the edge for both of us.

My aura field does not change. Any wrong movement and either of us could fall to our death. Miki's edge is more severe, a sharp drop, but it won't matter either way.

"Yes, I do see it," I say, my adrenaline building for this final showdown. "I see that Soren and I escaped the Fall Gauntlet and still aren't dead. I see a world that hasn't seen its gods and goddesses in millennia. I see a world in which the Crown controls its people. But the lynx sees so much more. It sees that it does not need gods or goddesses to win, only a human champion to fight with it."

I say it and my muscles contract with new strength.

Miki hisses. "You're no protector. You're a murderer just like me. Only one of us can succeed tonight!" Miki stands tall, more human than reptile now, and waves her arms in a specific formation like she is calling upon something. Her skeletal fingers spark with yellow-blue light, and her outline glows with some new kind of power. She takes a deep breath as electrical currents spread out from her heart, coursing through her arms to her crackling fingertips as lightning emerges and shoots straight at my chest.

This is it.

I hold my gem staff up and out, bracing myself for the shock, as her lightning bolt strikes my gem staff, which takes the brunt of the attack. I fight off the electricity's enduring power, sliding backward to the edge, my staff hot even through my gauntlets until it's over, and my gem staff crackles with the electrical energy I've now absorbed.

"PEASANT!" Miki screams, dashing at me, then rearing back to blast the most gigantic fireball I have ever seen out of her mouth as I swing my staff, which bursts with the kinetic power it's absorbed, back toward Miki's enlarged and mutated body.

Electricity and fire collide in an explosive mixture.

The brunt of the repelled attack smashes the black-tar salamander from hell in front of me, sweeping the chrysix up in a fiery torpedo and sending it off the edge. The mask pops off, and the flames burning the ancient tech are the last thing I see as I slide backward—the force of my strike returning its equal and opposite reaction—and go careening off the mountain's edge.

Darkness greets me.

So does water.

My body is sucked down. Down, down, down into a raging hot pool of water. It takes me a moment to realize that I've fallen into a rather deep hot spring. I plunge, then sink lower—it seems like forever—until gravity finally loosens its hold on me. My lungs, desperate for oxygen, revolt and push me to swim toward the surface. My body burns.

I reach the surface, gasping for breath, grasping for the edge, for life as if this is not real, and I've somehow cheated death. I cough and choke, holding the edge, needing to pull myself out of the heat. I clamber out, panicking, and collapse to the ground.

I'm in a black fury of hell, nauseous, dizzy, and slowly slipping into delirium. I remove my own mask as my neurons burn at my temples and consciousness slips away from me. Everything burns. I drag myself across the wet rocks away from the steam and heat.

Miki is dead, and I killed her.

A different pain sets in as guilt and misery claw at my battered mind and body. This fight feels different than the one with Dr. Fitz. I knew Miki, at least for a little while. I helped her with chores and lived in her spa. I didn't want it to happen like this, but I had to stop the chrysix.

The chrysix made me do it.

That's what I tell myself as I inch to higher ground away from the hot springs and finally lose consciousness.

EIGHT

"Benji? Benji, wake up," says a familiar voice that is neither Miki nor the chrysix. I battle the onslaught of pain shooting through my body and blink open heavy eyes as a round face swims into view. Lyaza's dark eyes swirl with questions as she looks into mine, as the dark sky above blurs and shadows fade to light. She and Miki have the same knowing eyes, the same searching gaze hungry for new knowledge.

Lyaza searches me for answers but only finds my body ripped of its spirit.

I don't know how or why she drags me back to her spa on some kind of solar powered slingbed, my mute and incapacitated body cradled in its mesh hammock, but she does.

She gives me water. She feeds me something sweet like honey. I want to vomit. My body is weak and bruised and my brain is fried. Was there anything I could have done differently? Could I have saved Miki in the end?

The hour trekking back to the spa is a mangled memory of passing out and waking up, the sun up and blaring, drying my clothes and bringing my lacerations and burns into excruciating focus.

I blink my eyes open, seeing Lyaza's childish face, the trauma she's already suffered at only thirteen, and my pain deepens knowing that I'm the cause of even more. She doesn't ask about Miki and I don't tell her. Maybe she already knows.

I look at my weather-beaten and bloody hands, examining all the pieces of myself I lost in the fight, everything that Miki … that the chrysix took from me. Why does it feel like the Fall Gauntlet will follow me wherever I go?

The spa attendants help me limp inside. I search nearby for my gem staff and mask but don't spot them anywhere. There's no way Lyaza didn't see them both when she found me. There's no way she doesn't know who I am by now, and I'm too tired to hide it anymore.

The attendants lead me to the bathroom. They help me strip my wet, sticky, blood-streaked clothes from my body as I stumble to the bathtub. Glimpsing myself in the mirror, I'm disturbed by what I see: a thin, slightly malnourished boy covered in welts and bruises. My hair is disheveled and plastered to my forehead. My muscles sag beneath a thin layer of skin that is pale from so many months indoors.

"Soren," I say, as the elderly men help lower me into the bathtub. "How is Soren?"

They say nothing.

I don't know if I'm even making sense or saying words. I just know that I want this pain to go away. I slip into the warm bathwater, and my blood stains it a shade of cherry. An aroma bomb diffuses, releasing smells of lavender and hibiscus, calming me and soothing my skin. It's not long before I drift off to sleep, fully surrendering to whatever treatments the attendants give to me.

The next time I wake up, I'm in a bed. Opening my eyes, I know the day has moved on. Soren is asleep on the same twin mattress I left him in. Lyaza must have moved my bed to be with him.

"Soren," I say, my voice shaky, my body starved for nourishment. He says nothing. Only his slow breathing shows me that he is still alive.

Light cuts through the window on the far wall, where the white linen curtain is half pulled back to show the sun setting behind the mountains. It looks like the most gigantic fireball I have ever seen. Just like that, visions of what happened last night return to me.

Lightning streaks down in violent bursts of yellow light.

A gigantic reptilian tail slams down like the hammer of the gods.

Water hot enough to boil skin wraps me in its deadly embrace.

I pass out again. The physical pain has dulled. I'm sure I was given some kind of sedative to numb the pain and let me heal. The emotional pain stabs at me like I'm lying on a bed of needles. I feel not myself, cruel and callous, an instrument of the Crown.

A murderer.

That's what Miki called me. That's what I am.

Soren wouldn't say so. All I want is to talk to my brother. This isn't at all how I thought my time with Miki and Lyaza would go, and my chest aches when I think about what it means. I'm terrified that the Dei will appear one day and decide to end everything, to squash the humans that no longer honor them. It's all my fault.

It takes a few days for me to gain back my strength and clarity. The attendants bring us soups and cold noodle dishes made from mashed black beans. They're the most delicious things I have ever tasted, and I let them know. I eat everything brought to me. I'm uneasy every time Lyaza visits us. I don't want to lie to her. She deserves to know.

Two days into my recovery, she brings up the topic herself. She starts by delivering my mask and gem staff to the room, laying them in the corner near Soren's things. She found them when she recovered me from the hot springs and brought them back with us.

When she sits cross-legged on the floor next to me at my bed, my heart thumps in my ears. My blisters burn and my forehead grows hot and feverish.

"I didn't think she would find it," Lyaza says.

I look at her, trying to read her expression. Is she devastated that her sister is gone? What will her life be like now? She's as stoic as ever.

"Find what?" I say, taking care to speak slowly.

"The chrysix mask," Lyaza says, her gaze fixed on me. "I know that you're the lynx, Benji. I know that you fought the chrysix, my sister, and won. I know that you killed Miki."

My heart weighs a thousand pounds then and sinks like a stone in my chest. Knocking other gauntlet challengers off the arena is one thing but hurting and killing people that are loved by other people in my life is another beast. I want to sink through the mattress and then the floor.

Lyaza watches me, silent expectation moving behind her eyes.

It seems like she wants me to say something, so I do. "I'm sorry, Lyaza. I tried to bring her back. I wanted to." My words fall limp like an uprooted weed.

"I wanted you to as well," Lyaza says, and her chest wells with what seems like sadness, regret even. "But that was before I knew she had the chrysix mask. She was the chosen one. Their spirits were aligned, and it's likely they wanted the same things."

I take a moment to let Lyaza's words sink in. Perhaps the chrysix and Miki were using each other, and their energies were too selfish, too out of sync to succeed.

"You and Miki, the lynx and the chrysix," Lyaza says. "You had to fight each other. I understand how the Fall Gauntlet works."

"So you think it was the only way?"

"You cannot deny the mask if it chooses you," Lyaza says, not really answering my question.

Shadows in the room grow taller and wider as the sun drops deeper behind the mountains. Soren snorts in his sleep. Moments pass in silence.

"Do you want to kill me?" I ask.

Lyaza stares at me, hesitating. Her eyes swirl like dark pools in an underwater cavern. I can't really see into them, but I need to know what's coming for Soren and me. "Right now, I need time to process what happened." Lyaza stands, then hesitating again, says, "I wanted to bring Miki back to reality, to life back here with me, but she was already lost. She would have burned an entire village to the ground if it would have brought our parents back."

"Would you not?" I ask. "Burn a village to the ground for your parents?"

Lyaza shakes her head. "No. I want to reunite with my parents too, but I would never take innocent lives in exchange for theirs."

"How come you seem so much older than thirteen?"

Lyaza inhales a sharp breath, like she holds more of the world's weight than I do. "Maybe I learned a lot from Miki, absorbed some of her misery, found ways to beat the pain before it could beat me."

"It's okay to feel the pain," I say, knowing its different forms, the serrated edges that stab and eviscerate, the agonizing aches that wake you from sleep and kiss you goodnight. Pain is a chameleon that never truly leaves your body.

"Do you really think your parents are still alive?" Lyaza asks.

The question is unexpected. I'm still thinking about how I killed Miki. If someone had ended Soren's life, I wouldn't be able to not hate them, much less look them in the eyes a few days later. I don't understand how Lyaza is so solemn about this, but then again, I don't know what happened with her parents, or about her relationship with them.

"I don't know," I say after some time.

"I always wonder," Lyaza says, steepling her fingers at her chin. "What if we get back to our parents, and they aren't the same people we remember?"

"I don't expect that they will be the same people," I say. "After everything they've been through, I'm sure they've changed a lot."

Lyaza looks away, tilts her head and sighs. "I just keep thinking, what if this is how it's supposed to happen? What if they're gone, and we're meant to move on?"

"I can't move on without knowing what's happened to them."

"So they're our passion and our pain," she says. "The reason we keep fighting."

I'm clenching my teeth, biting back a sudden rush of emotions I didn't know were there. Holding back tears, I wonder when the pain of losing people we love ends. Mom used to bring me soup when I was sick. She didn't care if she'd get sick, and she usually did. She always stepped into battle for Soren and me.

My chest aches and swells like the rising tide, and I'm unable to hold back the monstrous and ugly pain that wants to flee my body, like I fled the gauntlet days ago. Tears spring from my eyes as I try to clench them shut, as I try to cage the beast that claws for freedom. My mind conjures up images of Mom as I last saw her: defiant, brave, strong.

"It's okay to feel the pain," Lyaza says, mirroring my own advice.

So I do. I cry and release the pain that's been living inside me for so long. I don't know how long I feel the pain, but I feel lighter after.

"Is Soren ... okay?" I ask, finally able to make words again, my voice strained. "Has he woken up at all?"

Lyaza looks at my brother. "Not really, Benji. He gets better, then worse."

My eyes dart to Soren, a sudden fear rising in me. "What's happening to him?"

"I don't know," Lyaza says.

I wipe away tears with the thin blanket covering me. I need time to process too, I think.

"Get some rest," Lyaza says, walking to the door. "There's a doctor that I think will be able to help your brother, but the journey will be long. Since it seems like you'll be needing my help and we have a common enemy, I'll be coming with you."

Shock doesn't even begin to describe what I'm feeling.

Does Lyaza feel anything at all?

Great. Another doctor and another long journey ahead. "I want to sleep for a month," I say.

Lyaza slides the door open and turns to face me. She stifles a laugh. "I wish you could, but we don't have that kind of time."

"Why not?" There is something in Lyaza's tone that makes me sit up.

"Because people spotted a certain bear and lynx on the train. Many people know you're in Oajin. It's only a matter of time before they discover you're here."

I've barely had time to heal from the chrysix battle, and now I have to think about the next one? I didn't ask for this, and yet I don't seem to have a choice. "So, the Fall Gauntlet continues. I wasn't ready to face my brother, or the rat man in the sewers, and I certainly wasn't ready to fight your sister. I'll be ready for this next battle." I can already feel better blood circulation in my legs and the beginnings of grip strength in my hands.

Lyaza's smile is thin. "It's good to hear you say that because we might have our first visitor sooner than expected. Last night, the condor mask chose its new champion."

I hear Lyaza speak, but for a moment, I hear Miki's voice too, how she possessed the strength to go after what she wanted. How the mask corrupted her and she lost herself trying to save her parents.

The chrysix's deceitful voice echoes in my head, reminding me what the totem animals are capable of and the dangers that await us.

END OF BOOK THREE

YOU'VE BEEN CHOSEN

The revolution needs your voice now more than ever!
Please share your thoughts by leaving an honest review
for *The Fall Gauntlet Omnibus, Volume 1*. Your review helps
more readers discover this book.

SCAN ME!

Thank you for reading this Fall Gauntlet Omnibus, Volume 1 (Books 1 – 3). There's more to come!

www.jamerkel.com